I0614407

Reprint Publishing

FOR PEOPLE WHO GO FOR ORIGINALS.

www.reprintpublishing.com

"EXCUSE ME," SAID THE STRANGER, "BUT WE HAVE TO BE
VERY PARTICULAR HERE."

BIKEY
THE SKICYCLE
& OTHER TALES
of JIMMIEBOY

By
JOHN KENDRICK BANGS

Author of
"Uncle Sam Trustee," "Mr. Munchausen,"
"House Boat on the Styx," etc.

ILLUSTRATED BY PETER NEWELL

New York
RIGGS PUBLISHING COMPANY
MCMII

COPYRIGHT, 1902, BY
RIGGS PUBLISHING CO.

TABLE *of* CONTENTS

		PAGE
I.	Bikey the Skicycle	11
II.	The Imp of the Telephone	81
III.	Caught in Toy Town	161
IV.	Totherwayville, the Animal Town	179
V.	An Electrical Error	197
VI.	In the Brownie's House	213
VII.	Jimmieboy—and Something	231
VIII.	Jimmieboy's Fire Works	247
IX.	High-Jinks in the Barn	265
X.	Jimmieboy's Valentine	275
XI.	The Magic·Sled	291
XII.	The Stupid Little Apple Tree	309

ILLUSTRATIONS

"Excuse me" said the stranger, " but we have to
be very particular here"   -   See Frontispiece

Before him stood the Imp   -   -   Facing page ~~74~~ 78

"At last!" ejaculated the Imp   -   "   "   124

The Electric Custard   -   -   -   "   "   150

"No wonder it wouldn't say anything,"
he cried   -   -   -   -   "   "   ~~186~~ 194

"I'm very glad to see you Sharkey,"
said the Lobster   -   -   -   "   "   ~~234~~ 229

"Your ears would be frozen solid"   "   "   ~~270~~ 263

"Hullo! said his papa, where have you been?"   ~~298~~ 306

BIKEY THE SKICYCLE

BIKEY *the* SKICYCLE

I

HOW IT ALL CAME ABOUT

JIMMIEBOY'S father had bought him a bicycle, and inasmuch as it was provided with a bag of tools and a nickel plated bell the small youth was very much pleased with the gift.

"It's got rheumatic tires, too," he said, when describing it to one of his little friends.

"What's that?" asked the boy.

"Big pieces of hose pipe," said Jimmieboy. "They run all around the outside of the wheel and when you fill 'em up with wind and screw 'em up tight so's the wind can't get out, papa says, you can go over anything easy as a bird."

" I s'pose," said the little friend, "it's sort of like sailing, maybe. The wind keeps blowing inside o' those pipes and that makes the wheels go round."

" I guess that's it," returned Jimmieboy.

" But I don't see why they call 'em rheumatic," said the other boy.

" Nor I don't, either," said Jimmieboy, " unless it's because they move a little stiff at first."

It was not long, however, before Jimmieboy discovered that his father had made a mistake when he said that the pneumatic tire would enable a bicycle to ride over anything, for about a week later Jimmieboy tried to ride over the shaft of a lawn mower with his wheel, with disastrous results. The boy took a header, and while he himself was not hurt beyond a scratch or two and a slight shaking up, which took away his appetite, the wonderful rubber tire was badly battered. What was worse, the experience made Jimmieboy a little afraid of his new possession, and for some time it lay neglected.

A few nights ago, however, Jimmieboy's interest in his wheel was aroused once more, and to-day it is greater than ever, and it all came about in this way. His father and mother had gone out to make some calls and the youngster was spending a few minutes of solitude over a very fine fairy book that had recently been sent to him. While he was gazing at a magnificent picture of Jack slaying two giants with his left hand and throttling a dragon with his right, there came a sudden tinkling of a bell.

"Somebody's at the telephone," thought Jimmieboy, and started to go to it, when the ringing sound came again, but from a part of the house entirely away from the neighborhood of the telephone.

"Humph," said Jimmieboy. "That's queer. It isn't the telephone and it can't be the front door bell—I guess it's the——"

"It's me—Bikey," came a merry voice from behind the door.

"Who?" cried Jimmieboy.

"Bikey," replied the voice. "Don't you remember Bikey, who threw you over the lawn mower?"

Jimmieboy turned about, and sure enough there stood his neglected wheel.

"I hope you weren't hurt by your tumble," said the little bicycle standing up on its hind wheel and putting its treadles softly on Jimmieboy's shoulders, as if it were caressing him.

"No," said Jimmieboy. "The only thing was that it took away my appetite, and it was on apple pie day. It isn't pleasant to

14

feel as if you couldn't eat a thing with a fine apple pie staring you in the face. That was all I felt badly about."

"I'm sorry about the pie," returned the little bicycle "but glad you didn't flatten your nose or put your teeth out of joint, as you might easily have done. I knew a boy once who took a header just as you did, and after he got up he found that he'd broken the brim of his hat and turned a beautiful Roman nose into a stub nose."

"You mean snub nose, don't you?" asked Jimmieboy.

"No, I mean stub. Stub means more than snub. Snub means just a plain turn up nose, but stub means that it's not only turned up, but has very little of itself left. It's just a stub—that's all," explained the bicycle. "Another boy I knew fell so hard that he pushed his whole face right through to the back of his head, and you don't know

how queer it looks to see him walking backward on his way to school."

"I guess I was in great luck," said Jimmieboy. "I might have had a much harder
time than I did.

"I should say so," said the bicycle. "A
scratch and loss of appetite, when you might
just as easily have had your whole personal
appearance changed, is getting off very
cheap. But, I say, why didn't you turn
aside instead of trying to ride over that lawn
mower? Didn't you know you'd get yourself
into trouble?"

"Of course I didn't," said Jimmieboy.
"You don't suppose I wanted to commit
soozlecide, do you? I heard papa talking to
mamma about the rheumatic tires on his
bicycle, and he said they were great inven-
tions because they made the wheel boy—boy
—well, boy something, I don't remember
what."

"Boyant?" asked the little bicycle, scratching its cyclometer with its pedal.

"Yes—that was it," said Jimmieboy. "He said the rheumatic tires made the thing boyant, and I asked him what that meant. He said boyant was a word meaning light and airy—like a boy, you know, and that boyancy in a bicycle meant that it could jump over almost anything."

"That is so," said Bikey. "That's what they have those tires for, but they can't jump over a lawn mower—unless"——Here Bikey paused and glanced anxiously around. It was evident that he had some great secret in his mind.

"Unless what?" asked Jimmieboy, his curiosity at once aroused.

"Unless a patent idea of mine, which you and I could try if you wanted to, is good."

Bikey's voice sank into a whisper.

"There's millions in my idea if it'll work,"

he continued. " Do you see this? " he asked, holding up his front wheel. " This tire I have on is filled with air, and it makes me seem light as air—but it's only seeming. I'm heavy, as you found out when you tried to get me to jump over the lawn mower, but if I could only do a thing I want to you could go sailing over a church steeple as easily as you can ride me over a lawn."

" You mean to say you'd fly? " asked Jimmieboy, delighted at the idea.

" No—not exactly," returned Bikey. " I never could fly and never wanted to. Birds do that, and you can buy a bird for two dollars; but a bicycle costs you anywhere from fifty to a hundred, which shows how much more valuable bicycles are than birds. No, I don't want to fly, but I would like to float."

" On water? " asked Jimmieboy.

" No, no, no; in the air," said the little bicycle impatiently—" like a balloon.

18

Wouldn't that be fine? Anybody can float on the water, even an old cork; but when it comes to floating in the air, that's not only fun but it means being talented. A bicycle that could float in the air would be the finest thing in the world."

"That's very likely true," said Jimmieboy, "but how are you going to do it? You can't soar."

"Not with my tires filled with air," replied Bikey, "but if you'll take the hose from the gas stove and fasten one end to the supply valve of my tires, the other to the gas fixture, fill the tires up with gas and get aboard I'll bet you we can have a ride that'll turn out to be a regular sky-scraper."

It sounded like an attractive proposition, but Jimmieboy wanted to know something more about it before consenting to trifle with the gas pipe.

"What good'll the gas do?" he asked.

"Why don't you know that gas makes bal-
loons go up?" said Bikey. "They just cram
the balloon as full of gas as they can get it
and up she sails. That's my idea. Fill my
rubber tires with gas and up we'll go.
What do you say?"

"I'll do it," cried Jimmieboy with enthu-
siasm. "I'd love more than anything else to
go biking through the clouds, for to tell the
truth clouds look a great deal softer than
grocery carts and lawn mowers, and I
wouldn't mind running into one of them so
much. Skybicycling"——

"Pooh! What a term," retorted Bikey.
"Skybicycling! Why don't you use your
mind a little and call it skycycling?"

Jimmieboy laughed.

"Perhaps skycling would be better than
that," he suggested.

"Or skiking," smiled the little bicycle.
"If it works you know I'll be simply grand.

I'll be a sort of Christopher Columbus among bicycles, and perhaps I'll be called a skicycle instead of bicycle. Oh, it would be too beautiful!" he added, dancing joyously on his hind wheel.

"It will indeed," said Jimmieboy, "but let's hurry. Seems to me as if I could hardly wait."

"Me too," chuckled Bikey. "You go up and get the rubber tube, fasten it to the gas pipe, and inside of ten minutes we'll be off—if it works."

So Jimmieboy rushed off to the attic, seized a piece of rubber tubing that had been used to carry the supply of gas to his little nursery stove in the winter, and running back to where Bikey was waiting fastened it to the fixture in the hall.

"Now," said Bikey, unscrewing the cap of his pneumatic tire, "hold the other end there and we'll see how it goes."

21

Jimmieboy hastened to obey, and for five minutes watched his strange little friend anxiously.

" Feel any lighter? " he said.

" Yes," whispered Bikey, almost shivering with delight. " My front wheel is off the floor already. I think twenty feet more will be enough there, and when you've filled up the hind tire—ta—ta—ti—tum—ti—too— ha—ha! Then we'll go skiking."

The plan was followed out, and when both tires had taken in as much gas as they could hold Bikey called hoarsely to Jimmieboy :—

" Quick! Quick! Jump aboard or I'll be off without you. Is the door open? "

" No," said Jimmieboy, clambering into the saddle, after turning off the gas and screwing the caps firmly on both tires, " b—but the par—par—parlor window is."

" Good," cried Bikey. " We'll sail

22

through that! Give the right pedal a good turn; now—one—two—three—we're off!"

And they were off. Out of the hall they flew, through the parlor without touching the floor, and then sailed through the window out into the moonlight night.

"Isn't it great," cried Bikey, trembling with delight.

"Greatest that ever was," said Jimmie-boy. "But, hi! Take care, turn to the left, quick."

A great spike of some sort had loomed up before them.

"Excuse me," said Bikey, giving a quick turn. "I was so happy I wasn't looking where we were going. If you hadn't spoken we'd have got stuck on that church steeple sure enough."

II

WHEELING ON THE BIG RING OF SATURN

"HADN'T we better go a little higher?" asked Jimmieboy. "There's a lot of these tall steeples about here, and it wouldn't be any fun if we pricked a hole in one of these tires on a weather vane."

"We are going higher all the time," said Bikey. "There isn't a steeple in the world can touch us now. What we want to keep away from now are eagles and snow clad Alps."

"Ho! snow clad Alps," laughed Jimmieboy. "There aren't any Alps in America, they're all in Europe."

24

"Well, where are you? You don't suppose we've been standing still all this time, do you? If you'd studied your geography lessons as well as you ought to you'd be able to tell one country from another. You are wheeling directly over France now. In ten minutes we'll be over Germany, and in fifteen, if you turned to the south, you'd simply graze the top of Mont Blanc."

"Let's," said Jimmieboy. "I want to see a glazier."

"A what?" asked Bikey.

"A glazier," answered Jimmieboy. "It's a big slide."

"Oh, you mean a glacier," said Bikey, shaking all over with laughter. "I thought you meant a man to put in a pane of glass, and it struck me that Mont Blanc was a curious place to go looking for one. Shall we turn south?"

"If you don't mind," said Jimmieboy.

"Seems to me we might coast down Mont Blanc, and have a pretty good time of it."

"Oh, if that's what you're after, I won't do it," said Bikey. "Coasting isn't a good thing for beginners like you, particularly on the Alps. Take a hill of your own size. Furthermore, we haven't come out to explore the earth. I was going to take you off to the finest bicycle track you ever saw. I never saw it either, but I've seen pictures of it. It's a great level gold road running about another world called Saturn. We call it Saturn's ring down home, but I've ideas as to what it is."

"Seems to me I've heard papa speak of Saturn. It's got eight moons, I think he said. One for every day of the week, and two for Sunday," said Jimmieboy.

"That's the place," said Bikey. "You don't need a lamp on your wheel when you go out at night there. They've got moonlight to burn. If you'll pedal ahead now as hard as you can we can get there in time for one turn and then come back; and I tell you, my boy, that coming back will be glorious. It will be down grade all the way."

" How far off is Saturn? " asked Jimmieboy.

" I don't know," returned Bikey, " but it's a long walk from your house. The ring is 18,350 miles from Saturn itself. That's why I think it's a good place for bicycling. Nobody'd take an ice cart or a furniture truck that far just to get in the way of a wheelman, and then as it doesn't go anywhere but just round and round and round, they're not likely to have trolley cars on it. It doesn't pay to run a trolley car nowheres."

It all seemed beautifully reasonable, and Jimmieboy's curiosity grew greater and greater as he pedalled along. Up and on they went, passing through huge fleecy masses of clouds, now and again turning to

27

one side to avoid running into strange little bits of stars, so small that they seemed to be nothing but islands in the ocean of the sky, and far too small to be seen on the earth.

"We can stop and rest on one of those if you want to, Jimmieboy," said Bikey; "are you tired?"

"Not at all," Jimmieboy answered. "Seems to me I could go on this way forever. It's easy as lying down and going to sleep."

Bikey chuckled.

"What are you laughing at?" said Jimmieboy.

"Nothing," said Bikey. "When you said it was easy as sleeping I thought of something—that was all."

"Dear me," said Jimmieboy, ruefully. "I am awake, ain't I? This isn't like all the other experiences, is it?"

28

"Not at all," laughed Bikey. "Your other adventures have been quite different. But, I say, we're getting there. I can see five moons ahead already."

"I can see six," cried Jimmieboy, quite elated. "Yes, six—and—one more."

"You've got nearly the whole set, as the boy said when he came to the other boy's Nicaragua page in the stamp album. There are only eight altogether—only I think your seventh is Saturn itself."

"It must be," said Jimmieboy. "It's got a hello around it."

"What's that?" asked Bikey.

"I forgot," said Jimmieboy. "You never went to Sunday school, and so of course you don't know what a hello is. It's a thing like a gold hoople that angels wear on their heads."

"I'll have to get one," said Bikey. "I heard somebody say I was an angel of a bicycle. I don't know what she meant, though. What is an angel?"

"It's a—a—good thing with wings," said Jimmieboy.

"Humph!" said Bikey, "I'm afraid I'm not one of those. Don't they ever have wheels? I'm a good thing, but I haven't any wings."

"I never heard of an angel with wheels," said Jimmieboy. "But I suppose they come. Angels have everything that's worth having."

Bikey was silent. The idea of anything having everything that was worth having was too much for him to imagine, for bicycles have very little imagination.

"I wish I could be one," he said wistfully, after a moment's silence. "It must be awfully nice to have everything you want."

Jimmieboy thought so, too, but he was too much interested in getting to Saturn to say anything, so he, too, kept silent and pedalled away as hard as he could. Together and happily they went on until Jimmieboy said :—

"Bikey, what's that ahead? Looks like the side of a great gold cheese."

"That," Bikey answered, "is exactly what you think it is. It's the ring of Saturn, and, as the saying goes, for biking Saturn is quite the cheese. In two minutes we'll be there."

And in two minutes they were there. In less, in fact, for hardly eight seconds had passed before a great, blinding light caused Jimmieboy to close his eyes, and when he had opened them again he and Bikey were speeding along a most beautiful road, paved with gold.

"I thought so," said Bikey, "we're on the ring. And isn't it smooth?"

"It's like riding on glass," said Jimmieboy. And then they stopped short.

A peculiar looking creature had stopped them. It was a creature with a face not unlike that of a man, and a body like a man's, but instead of legs it had wheels like a bicycle. If you can imagine a Centaur with a body like a bicycle instead of a horse you will have a perfect mental picture of this strange creature.

"Excuse me," said the stranger, "but we have to be very particular here. Where do you come from?"

"Earth," said Bikey.

"All right," said the stranger. "Move on, I'm a Saturn policeman and so many wheelmen from the Sun and the Moon and Jupiter have caused disturbances of late that we have had to forbid them coming. You are the only Earth people who have been here, and of course are not included in our rules, but I will have to go along with you to see that you do not break any of them."

"We're very glad to meet you," said Bikey, "and if you'll tell us your rules we will be very glad to obey them."

"Well," said the creature with wheels instead of legs, "the first rule is that nobody shall ride a wheel standing on his head. There was a person over here from Mars last week who actually put his head in the saddle and wheeled his pedals with his hands."

"How utterly absurd!" said Jimmieboy.

"Wasn't it?" said the Saturnian; "and my! how mad he got when I interfered—asked whether this was a free country and if anybody had rights, and all sorts of stuff like that. Now there's another rule we have, and that is that coasting backward cannot be permitted. We used to allow that until a man from Jupiter ran slap bang into another man who lived at the extreme end of the handle of the Great Dipper, who was

33

coasting backward from the other direction. They came together so hard that we couldn't get 'em apart, and we have had to keep 'em here ever since. They can't be separated, and the Dipper man won't go to Jupiter, and the Jupiter man won't go to Dipperville—consequently they stay here. They're a fearful nuisance, and it all came from coasting backward."

"It's a very good rule," said Jimmieboy, "but in our world I don't think we'd need a rule like that, because, while our bicycle riders do lots of queer things, I don't think they'd do that."

"I hope not," said the Saturnian, "because there isn't any use in it, any more than in that other trick our visiting bicyclists try to play here. They take those bicycles built for two, you know, and have what they call tugs of war with 'em. One fellow takes the hind wheel and the other the front wheel,

and each begins to work for all he is worth
to pull the other along. We had to stop
that, too, because the last time they did it
the men were so strong that the bar was
pulled apart and both tuggers went flying
off on one wheel so fast that they have never
managed to get back—not that we want
them back, but that we don't want people to
set bicycling down as a dangerous sport. It
means so much to us. We get all our money
from our big ring here; bicyclists come from
all parts of the universe to ride around it,
and as they pay for the privilege why we get
millions of dollars a year, which is divided
up among the people. Consequence is, nobody has to do any work and we are all
happy. You can see for yourself that it
would be very bad for us if people gave it up
as dangerous."

"Very true," said Bikey, "and now we
know the rules I suppose we can go ahead."

35

"Yes," said the policeman, "only you must go to the Captain's office and get a permit. It'll cost you $2,000 for one season."

" Two thousand dollars? " echoed Jimmieboy, aghast.

" That's what I said," said the policeman.

" But," said Jimmieboy, ruefully, " I haven't got more than five cents with me."

" Then," said the policeman, " you can get a permit for five cents' worth—that's one-forty thousandth part of a season."

" And how long is a season? " asked Jimmieboy.

" Forty thousand years," said the policeman. " You can ride a year for five cents."

Bikey laughed.

" That'll be long enough," he said. " And where can I find the Captain? "

" I'm him," said the Saturnian. " Give me the five cents and it will be all right."

So Jimmieboy handed over his nickel, and

in a moment he and Bikey were speeding along over a beautiful golden road so wide that he could not see the other side of it, and stretching on and on to the fore for thousands of miles.

III

A SUDDEN STOP AT THE TYRED INN

"THIS is a great place," said Bikey as they sped along. "I've coasted on pretty much every kind of coasting thing there is, and I think I never struck anything like this before. It beats the North Pole all hollow."

"You never coasted on the North Pole, did you?" queried Jimmieboy.

"Oh, didn't I just!" laughed Bikey. "It's made of ice, that North Pole is, and it's so slippery that you can even slide up it —that's awful slippery, when you come to think of it—and as for coming down, well, you'd almost think you were falling off a roof."

38

" But, wasn't it dangerous? " asked Jimmieboy.

" Not at all," laughed Bikey. " Sliding up you run into the air, and that isn't very hard, and coming down you land in a great snow bank—but this place here is much pleasanter, because it's warmer, and you don't have to exert yourself. That's the great thing about this track. We aren't going at all, though we seem to be—it's the track that makes my wheels go round. It's just a-whizzing, this track is, but we are standing perfectly still. If you should step off on to the road you'd whizz back out of sight in two seconds."

" Well, I won't step off, then," said Jimmieboy a little fearfully; " I don't want to be left up here all by myself."

Silently they went on for at least five minutes, when what should they see before them but a great stone wall, built solidly across the road.

"Hi!" cried Bikey. "Put on the brake —hurry up."

"There's isn't one," shrieked Jimmieboy. "I—b—bub—busted it on the lawn mower the day of the accident."

"Back pedal then—back pedal," roared Bikey.

"C—can't gug—get my feet on 'em, they're going so fast," cried Jimmieboy.

"Then p—pup—punk—puncture my tire —take a nail or a pin or anything—or we'll be dashed to pieces."

"Huh! haven't gug—got a nail or a pup— pin or anything," wept Jimmieboy.

"Then we are lost," said Bikey; but just then his tires punctured themselves and they came to a full stop two feet from the stone wall and directly in front of a little hotel, from the front door of which swung a bright red sign on which was the following inscription :—

40

THE TYRED INN

FOR

THE TIRED OUT.

" My! " ejaculated Bikey as he and Jimmieboy tumbled in a heap before the inn. " That was the narrowest escape I ever had. If we hadn't stopped we'd have been smashed all to bits—leastways I would have—you might have cleared the wall all right."

" Good morning, Biklemen," said a fat, pudgy little old fellow, appearing in the door way of the inn and bowing profoundly.

" What's that you say? " asked Bikey looking up. " I didn't catch that last word."

" Biklemen," repeated the fat little fellow. " It's a word I invented myself to save time and it signifies gentlemen who ride bicycles.

Instead of saying 'good morning, gentlemen who ride bicycles,' I say 'good morning, biklemen, is there anything I can do for you?'"

"Well, I should say there was," retorted Bikey. "Just look at my tires, will you? There are twenty-six punctures in the front one and eighteen in the hind one. I should think you'd have better sense than to sprinkle the road with tacks in this way."

"Why, what an ungrateful creature you are," cried the landlord of the Tyred Inn, for that was who the pudgy little old fellow was. "If it hadn't been for those tacks I'd like to know where you'd be at this moment. You'd have smashed into that stone wall and busted yourself and your rider all to pieces."

"That's so, Bikey," said Jimmieboy. "Those tacks saved our lives."

"Of course they did," said the landlord. "And even if you had a right to growl about

42

'em, you haven't any right to growl at me because the government compels me to keep that part of the road sprinkled with 'em."

"Really?" asked Bikey. "Queer law that, isn't it?"

"I don't see why you think that," replied the landlord. "Is it a queer law which results in the saving of people's lives?"

"No; but the way to save people's lives would be to remove that stone wall," said Bikey. "And that's the thing that makes this place dangerous."

"I don't like to be impolite to biklemen," said the landlord, "but I must say that you don't know what you are talking about. Do you suppose I am in business for fun?"

"I don't see what that has to do with it," said Bikey, ruefully regarding his tires, which looked for all the world like porous plasters would look if they were sold by the yard.

"Well, I'll show you in ten seconds," said

43

the landlord. " Do you see this inn? I presume you do, though there seems to be so little that you see that I have my doubts. Well, this inn is run, not because I think it's a game I'm playing, but because I'm after money. Now, this inn wouldn't earn a cent of money if biklemen didn't stop here. See that? "

" Yes," said Bikey. " That's plain enough, but that doesn't account for the tacks or the stone wall."

" Yes, it does, too," retorted the landlord. " I ran this inn two years before that stone wall was built, and I paid the government $500 a week for being allowed to do it, but nobody ever stopped. Every bikleman in the universe went coasting by here and never a one stopped in, so I never got a cent and was paying $26,000 a year to the government into the bargain. Of course I complained to the Secretary of the Interior, and he just laughed me off; said it wasn't his

44

fault; that I ought to do something myself
to make 'em stop, and that is how I came to
build the stone wall. They've got to stop
now. See that?"

"Yes," said Bikey, "I see. And did you
begin to make money?"

"Well, rather," said the landlord. "The
first day after that was built a lot of biklemen from the Moon came over here and they
ran plumb into that wall. Five out of eight
broke their legs, two broke their arms and
one of 'em got off with a cracked nose, but
every one of 'em had to stay here two months
at $10 a day apiece, and, of course, their
families had to visit 'em, and they paid from
$5 to $8 apiece, and then I charged 'em all
for medical services, and altogether things
began to look up. I cleared $7 a week
steady. But they were a mean crowd. In
spite of all the good treatment they got, as
soon as they got well they made a complaint
against that wall, said it was an outrage,

45

and the government said it must come
down.

" ' All right,' said I to the Secretary.
"But if that wall comes down I go out of
the hotel business, and you can whistle for
your $500 a week. He didn't like that a bit,
the Secretary didn't, because his salary depended on the money I paid. Being Secretary of the Interior he got a commission on
hotel taxes, and as mine was the only hotel
in Saturn, shutting it up meant that he was
ruined."

" You had him there," laughed Bikey.

" I rather guess so," smiled the landlord,
" and he knew it. Still I was easy with him.
I didn't want to have people making com-
plaints all the time, so I said that while the
stone wall had come to stay, I'd pave the
street for two hundred yards in front of it
with cat teasers."

" What? " cried Jimmieboy.

" Cat   teasers,"   said   the   landlord.

"Didn't you ever hear of cat teasers? They're small square pieces of zinc with prickers on 'em. City people generally put 'em on top of their back yard fences so that Patti cats "——

"Excuse me," asked Bikey. "What cats?"

"Patti cats and De Reszke cats—the kind that sing, you know," explained the landlord. "They put 'em on their back yard fences so that these operatic felines would not be able to sit down there and sing and keep them awake all night; but the scheme didn't work. I had an idea that the cat teasers would puncture the bicycle wheels in time to stop 'em, and they did, but they interfered with people on foot as well, and after these people got lockjaw from puncturing their feet on my pavement I took it up and suggested sprinkling the roadway twice a day with tacks. This satisfied the Secretary, and a law was passed compelling

47

me to do it, and I do. How it works you have seen for yourselves."

"That's true," said Bikey, ruefully.

"Well, it saved me," said Jimmieboy.

"But how are we ever to get home?" asked Bikey.

"Oh, as for that," returned the landlord, "gather yourselves together and come inside. I think I can fix you out very shortly, and it won't cost you more than $800."

"Come on, Bikey," said Jimmieboy, "I'd sort of like to see the inside of this house, anyhow."

"I haven't got any $800," snapped Bikey.

"Oh, never mind about that," laughed the landlord. "I run a banking business here, too. I'll lend you all you want. Come in."

And so they went into the "Tyred Inn for the Tired Out," and a most remarkable place they found it to be.

IV

THE TYRED INN

THE entrance to the Tyred Inn and the parlors and rooms of that extraordinary place were quite like those of any other roadside hotel, but the method of conducting it and the singular things that were to be found in it made Jimmieboy's brief stay there an experience long to be remembered. The bicycle idea was carried out in everything. If you wanted a bell boy you had to ring a bicycle bell. In place of an elevator or staircase they had a spiral pathway running up from the centre of the hall to the roof, upon which guests could either walk or ride, an electric bicycle built for two being provided for

49

those who did not care to walk up, the elevator boy sitting on the front seat and managing the apparatus.

From the parlor there came the most beautiful strains of music, as from a fine brass and string orchestra, all of which was managed by the merest bit of a midget sitting astride of a safety and working the pedals, which in turn worked the great musical instrument that occupied the whole of the lower end of the room. Upon the walls were all sorts of curious pictures, and for a decoration of the ceiling there were automatic frescoes presenting a constantly moving bicycle scene. For instance, instead of a series of groups of rosebuds and cupids, there were about a hundred little plaster wheelmen racing about the edge of the ceiling, and every once in a while one of these would take a header, flying immediately back to his saddle again, however, and continuing on his way until the clockwork by which the frescoes were run forced him to take the header all over again. On and around they raced incessantly, and so varied were the things that they did that it did not seem to Jimmieboy as if he could remember half of them in case he should ever want to tell his father or his brothers about it afterward.

"That's a fine ceiling, isn't it?" asked the landlord, with a grin, as Jimmieboy gazed overhead, his mouth wide open in wonderment.

"I should say so," replied the boy, delightedly. "I wish I could have a ceiling like that in my room."

"Nonsense," said Bikey. "You'd soon get tired of it. It wouldn't take long for a ceiling like that to drive a man crazy."

"That's so," put in the landlord. "But there are lots of things that would drive a man crazy that wouldn't drive a boy crazy—

51

like trumpets and whistles. When it comes
to things like that, boys are much stronger
than men. I've known a boy of five to stand
banging on a drum for seven hours, when his
father couldn't stand it for seven minutes.
Nobody need go crazy over my bicycle ceiling though," continued the landlord. "I
just press a button and it's all over—see?"

As the little man spoke he pressed a button on the side wall, and instantly the fresco
bicycles stopped moving, the little plaster
wheelmen jumped off and threw themselves
down upon the soft grassy borders of the
painted roadside and all was still. Then the
landlord pressed another button and they
jumped up, mounted again and the race began once more.

"That's my own invention," said the landlord, "and it's a very popular feature of my
house. It brings children here. When the
mothers of this neighborhood want to go off

wheeling, and there's nobody to look after the children, they bring them here and leave them with me, and they're as good as pie as long as that ceiling goes. That's another of my ways of making money. I charge fifty cents an hour for letting the youngsters in here, and it's a very poor sort of a day that I don't clear $40 on my kid account."

"I should think so," said Jimmieboy in a superior sort of way. "I think that if I were a child I should like to spend a day here myself."

The landlord looked at Jimmieboy with an amused expression.

"Say, Mr. Bike," he whispered to Bikey. "What does he think he is, a telegraph pole? He said if he was a child. Isn't he a child?"

"Yes," laughed Bikey, "but he is a little old for his age, you know. Had lots of experience."

"Ha—I see," said the landlord. Then he turned to Jimmieboy again and said:—

"Now, Mr. Man, if you'll accompany me up stairs I'll show you my pantry."

"Good," said Jimmieboy. "I must say I'm pretty hungry, and a pantry is just the sort of thing I'd like to see."

Mounting the "bikevator," as the printed sign over it called the arrangement that took guests to the upper floors, the party was soon transferred to the landing above. The landlord, after assisting Jimmieboy to dismount, walked to the end of a long corridor and, taking a bunch of keys from his pocket, unlocked and opened a little door.

"Come in," he said, as he disappeared through the door. "I have to keep the pantry locked."

Jimmieboy and Bikey entered as they were bid, and the landlord closed the door after them. The place was dimly lighted, but on the shelves, that rose one above another from floor to ceiling, all sorts of

54

curious looking bottles and cakes and pies and biscuits could be seen, and Jimmieboy's mouth watered at the sight.

" What'll you have? " asked the landlord. " An air cake or a piece of fresh pneumatic mince pie? "

" A little of both," said Jimmieboy.

" Or a bite of my gutta percha gum? " suggested the landlord.

" Well, it's hard to say," said Jimmieboy. " Indeed, I don't know what an air cake or a pneumatic mince pie is, nor did I ever hear of gutta percha gum."

" I know that mighty well," laughed the landlord. " Nobody ever heard of these patent dainties of mine, but they're the best things for the digestion you ever saw, and they last forever. If people could only train themselves to eat my food they'd be able to save money in two ways—bakers' bills and doctors' bills.

55

"I don't quite understand," said Jimmie-boy.

"One of my pneumatic mince pies will show you in a jiffy," returned the landlord. "One pie if properly cared for will last a lifetime"—

"Not with a real live boy in the house it won't," said Jimmieboy, positively.

"That may be all very true," said the landlord, "but if the real live boy ate one of those pies he would cease to be a real live boy. You see this pie is made of rubber, and all you've got to do is to blow it up with an air pump and serve it."

"But you called it mince pie," said Jimmieboy, very much disgusted.

"Well, it's my pie," said the landlord. "I guess I've got a right to call it what I please."

"But you said it saved doctors' bills," put in Bikey, who was no better pleased with this absurd invention than was Jimmieboy.

"And I said right," said the landlord, with a self-satisfied smile. "It's just this way:—If you eat mince pie it gives you indigestion and you have to send for the doctor, and then you get a bill for several dollars. Now, with my pie it's different. You can't eat it, and therefore you can't get indigestion, and you don't have to send for a doctor. Wherefore, as I said, it saves doctors' bills. This is the latest make—I make a new kind every year, just as the bicycle makers make new wheels every year. A 1902 safety pneumatic mince pie costs $2 a 1901 pie I sell for $1.50."

"And what is the difference?" asked Jimmieboy, beginning to be amused.

"The air in this year's pie is fresher, that's all," said the landlord.

"I suppose your air biscuits are of the same kind?" asked Bikey.

"Yes," said the landlord, "except that I flavor 'em. If you're fond of vanilla, or strawberry, or any other flavor, I perfume the air that is pumped into them. They're very nice."

"What are those things on the top shelf?" asked Jimmieboy. "They look like sausages."

"They are sausages. I make 'em out of old tires, and they are very good and solid. Then, over there in the icebox, I have rubber steaks and chickens—in fact, all kinds of pneumatic food. You have no idea how well they last, and how good they are for the digestion—if you could only get used to them. That's the greatest trouble I have, getting people used to them."

"Don't you have any real good food here?" asked Bikey.

"Real? Why, my dear fellow," ejaculated the landlord, "what could you ask more real than those rubber viands? You could drop a railway engine on one of those rubber sausages and it would be just as solid as ever."

"But you can't live on air!" protested Jimmieboy.

"No more can you live without it," said the landlord, unlocking the door and opening it, some disappointment manifested in his countenance. "If you will come up to the hospital now, sir," he added, addressing Bikey, "I'll see what can be done to repair your wounds. I am sorry you do not seem to appreciate the good things in my larder."

"We'd appreciate 'em if we could see the good of 'em," said Jimmieboy. "What on earth can you do with a rubber mince pie besides not eat it?"

"Oh! as for that, you might use it for a football," retorted the landlord sadly, as he locked the door behind them and started down the corridor to the hospital room.

"I call it the hospital room," said he,

" although I am aware that doesn't describe
it. We don't take care of horses there, but
as yet nobody has invented a word like
bikepital, and so I do not use it. I have ap-
plied for a patent on that word, however,
and as soon as I get it we'll change the
name."

With these words they entered the hospital, and if the pantry was queer the hospital was a marvel.

V

IN THE HOSPITAL AND HOME AGAIN

"COME right in," said the landlord, stepping into the hospital. "We'll fix Bikey up in
a jiffy, and as for young Mr. Jimmieboy,
we'll see what can be done to improve his
appetite for our gutta percha pies."

Jimmieboy glanced apprehensively at the
old gentleman. He did not like the tone in
which the remark was made.

"Thank you, Mr. Landlord," he said,
after thinking for a moment, "but you
needn't bother about me. I can get along
very well without liking them. The kind of
pies that we have at home are plenty good

61

enough for me, and I don't really care to like yours, thank you." Jimmieboy had tried to be at least polite. The landlord laughed unpleasantly.

"Humph!" he sneered, "that doesn't make any difference to us. Article number seven, paragraph sixty-three, of the hotel laws of Saturn requires that you SHALL like the food we serve at this hotel, whether you want to or not. Therefore, what you want or don't want to like cuts no figure here. You will have to be operated upon, and that portion of your anatomy which does not welcome the best pneumatic pie that ever was made will be removed."

Jimmieboy immediately perceived that he was in trouble, for the landlord spoke with great determination and, what was more, had locked the door behind him, so that the boy was practically a prisoner. Escape seemed impossible, and yet escape he must, for no one could relish the idea of becoming a patient at the Bicycle Hospital. To gain time to think, he observed as civilly as he could :—

"It seems to me, Mr. Landlord, that that is a curious law. Just because a traveller doesn't like the food at your hotel he's got to go to a hospital and stay there until he does like it. Isn't that a trifle queer?"

"Nothing queer about it at all," retorted the landlord savagely. "Nothing queer about it at all. Naturalest law in all the world. I'm not in business for fun, as I've already told you, and if I left any stone unturned to compel people to like my house I should be ruined. My guests have got to like everything, including me—I, myself, see? When I pay a big tax to the government for the privilege of doing business the government has got to do something to help me on in that business, and, fortunately for us, in Saturn we've got a government that is just chock full of justice and common sense.

" When I first started up here nobody liked the food I served, and after coming here once most of them never came again. Ruin was staring me in the face, so I went to the capital and I told the government that they had to do something for me, and they did. They passed an act compelling people to like my food under penalty of $500 a dislike, or six months in my hospital, where I am authorized to regard them as patients. Now you can take your choice. You don't like the pie, you don't like the sausage, you don't like the rubber chops and the bicycle saddle stew you look upon with disfavor. There are four things you don't like.

" Now you can do any one of three things. Eat all four of these dishes, pay a fine of $2,000 or stay here in the hospital and undergo a course of treatment. I don't care which. There's one thing certain. I'm not going to let you out of this place until you like everything about it."

Jimmieboy glanced uneasily at Bikey, who was leaning carelessly against the wall as if he were not at all bothered by the situation.

" But I've got to go to school to-morrow, Mr. Landlord," he put in. " Can't you let me off long enough to finish my term at school, and then when vacation comes maybe I'll come back? "

" No siree! " ejaculated the landlord. " I know what you are up to. You're nothing but a boy, and boys don't like schools any better than you like my pneumatic pies. You stay right here."

" Oh, tell him you like 'em, Jimmieboy," put in Bikey. " Tell him they beat mince all holler and pumpkin isn't in it with 'em.

Tell him life would be a barren waste and every heart full of winter if it wasn't for 'em. Pile it on and let's get out. I'm getting nervous."

"Well, so they are in a way," said Jimmieboy. "The fact is, they're the finest pies ever made."

The landlord's face brightened up.

"To eat?" he asked eagerly.

"N-n-o," stammered Jimmieboy. "Not to eat—but to play football with or to use for punching bags."

The landlord froze up immediately.

"That settles your case," he snapped. "I'll put you in the violent ward and to-morrow morning we'll begin a course of treatment that will make you wish you'd liked 'em from the beginning. And now for you, sir," the landlord added severely, turning to Bikey. "How about you and my pneumatic pies?"

"Oh," said Bikey, with a joyful fling of his right pedal. "I simply adore those pies. Indeed, if there's anything I love in the world it is gutta percha food. Have you any rubber neck clams?"

The landlord beamed approval. "You are a bikleman of sense," said he. "I will order up a pneumatic rhubarb at once."

Bikey's saddle turned pale.

"Oh, please don't trouble yourself, Mr. Landlord," he said, pulling himself together. "I—ah—I should love to have it, for if there is one thing in the world I love more than rheumatic pneubarb—I mean rheubarbic pneumat pie—I don't know what it is, but my doctor has ordered me not to touch it for a year at least. 'Mr. Bike,' said he the last time I saw him, 'you are killing yourself by eating piebarb roobs—I mean roobarb pies—they are too rich for your tubes, Mr. Bike,' were his precise

67

words. And he added that if I didn't quit eating them my pedals would be full of gout and that even my cyclometer would squeak."

"Under the circumstances," said the landlord, with an approving nod at Bikey, "I shall not take it amiss if you refuse to eat them. But your young friend here must remain and be treated. Meanwhile, I shall have your wounds repaired and let you go. Mr. Jimmieboy will be sent forthwith to the violent ward."

"Serves him good and right," Jimmieboy was appalled to hear Bikey reply. Here he was off in a strange, wild place, in the hands of an enemy, who threatened him with all sorts of dreadful things, and his only friend had gone back on him.

"Bikey!" said he, reproachfully.

"Served you right," roared Bikey. "Not to like the good gentleman's pies. Your father has told you again and again to always like what is put before you. You impolite child, you!"

Jimmieboy's pride alone kept him from bursting into tears, and he sorrowfully permitted himself without further resistance to be led away into the violent ward of the Inn Hospital.

"To think that he should go back on me!" the boy sighed as he entered the prison. "On me who never did him any harm but break his handlebars and bust his tires unintentionally."

But Jimmieboy, in his surprise and chagrin had failed to note the wink in Bikey's cyclometer, which all the time that he had been speaking was violently agitating itself in an effort to attract his attention and to let him know that his treachery was not real, but only seeming.

"Now," said the landlord kindly to Bikey, as Jimmieboy was led away, "let us attend

to you. I'll call the doctor. Doctor Pump!"
he added, calling the name loudly in a shrill
voice.

"Here, sir," replied the head physician,
running in from an adjoining room.

"Here's a chap who likes air pies so much
that his doctor forbids him to eat them. I
wish you'd fix him up at once," said the
landlord.

"He must be insane," said Dr. Pump,
"I'll send him to the asylum."

"Not I!" cried Bikey. "I'm merely
punctured."

"His wheels have gone to his head," said
Dr. Pump, feeling the pulse in Bikey's
pedals.

"Nonsense," said Bikey. "Impossible.
I haven't any head."

"H'm!" returned Dr. Pump, scratching
his chin. "Very true. In making my diag-
nosis I had failed to observe the fact that

you are an ordinary brainless wheel. Let me look at your tires."

Bikey held them out.

" Do you prefer homeopathic or allopathic treatment? " asked Dr. Pump. " We are broadminded here and give our patients their choice."

" What difference does it make in the bill? " asked Bikey.

" None," said Dr. Pump, grandly. " It is merely a difference in treatment. If you wish homeopathic treatment we will cure your tires, which seem to be punctured, with a porous plaster, since like cures like under that system. If, on the other hand, you are an allopath, we will pump you full of rubber."

" I think I prefer what they call absent treatment," said Bikey, meekly. " Can't you cure me over the telephone? I'm a Christian Scientist."

71

They had never heard of this at Saturn, so Bikey was compelled to submit to one of the two other courses of treatment, and he wisely chose the porous plaster to cure his puncture, since that required merely an external application, and did not involve his swallowing anything which might later have affected his general health.

Meanwhile poor Jimmieboy was locked up in the violent ward. It was a long low-ceiled room filled with little cots, and the lad found no comfort in the discovery that there were plenty more patients in the room.

"Why, the room's full, isn't it?" he said, as he entered.

"Yes," replied the bicycle attendant, who had shown him in. "In fact, everybody who comes to this house ends up here. Somehow or other, nobody likes the landlord's food, and nobody ever has money enough along to pay the fine. It is curious how little money bicyclists take along with them when they are out for a ride. In all my experience I haven't encountered one with more than a thousand dollars in his pocket."

" How long does one have to stay here? " asked Jimmieboy.

" Until one likes the food," said the attendant. " So far nobody has ever got out, so I can't say how long they stay in years."

Again the boy's heart sank, and he crawled into his cot, wretched in spirit and wholly unhappy.

" I've given you a bed by the window," said the attendant, " because the air is fresher there. The landlord says you are the freshest boy he ever met, and we have arranged the air accordingly. I wouldn't try to escape if I were you, because the window looks out on the very edge of the ring of Saturn, and it's a jump of about 90,000,000 miles to anything solid. The jump is easy,

73

but the solid at the other end is very, very hard."

Jimmieboy looked out of the window, and immediately drew back, appalled, for there was nothing but unfathomable space above, below, or beyond him, and he gave himself up to despair.

But the boy had really reckoned without his friend Bikey, who was as stanch and true as ever, as Jimmieboy was soon to find out.

He had lain in his little bed barely more than an hour, when from outside the window there came a whisper:—" Hi, there, Jimmieboy!"

Jimmieboy got up on his elbow to listen, but just then the door opened and Dr. Pump, accompanied by the landlord, walked in. So he lay back and the words at the window were not repeated.

Dr. Pump walked to the side of Jimmieboy's cot.

" Well, young man," said he, " what do you think of air pies up here, now? "

" They're bully," said Jimmieboy, weakly, and resolved to give in.

" H'm," said Dr. Pump. " Bad case, this. I can't say whether of insanity or compulsion. There's only one course. We'll order a pie. If he's insane he'll eat it. If he is acting under compulsion "——

" I won't eat it," roared Jimmieboy, springing up from his pillow. " I won't; I won't; I won't. I'll take cod liver oil on my strawberries first! "

His was evidently an awful case, for immediately Dr. Pump, the nurse and the landlord and every patient in the place fled from the room, shrieking with terror.

" Good for you! You've scared them silly," whispered the voice at the window. " Now, Jimmieboy, hurry. Jump out. I'll catch you and we'll be off. Be quick, for they'll be back in a moment. Jump! "

"Who are you!" cried Jimmieboy, for he was still the same cautious little traveller.

"Bikey! I only went back on you to help you!" he said. "Jump!"

And then the door opened again, and the landlord and Dr. Pump and the nurses and all the patients and a platoon of policemen crashed into the room.

"Catch him, quick!" cried the landlord. But Jimmieboy had already jumped, landing upon the friendly saddle of Bikey. In an instant he found himself speeding away through space.

"Are we still on Saturn?" he gasped.

"Not we!" cried Bikey. "That place is too hot for us. We're not on anything. I'm simply tumbling through the clouds and whirring my wheels for fun. I like to see the wheels go round. Don't bother. We'll land somewhere."

76

" But," cried Jimmieboy, " where? "

And then there was a crash. Bikey made no reply, but——

* * * * * * *

" Here," said a well known and affectionate voice.

" Where's here? " asked Jimmieboy, faintly, opening his eyes and gazing up into a very familiar face.

" You interrupted me, my son," remarked the owner of the familiar face. " I was about to say, ' Here now, Jimmieboy, this business of falling out of bed has got to stop.' This is the fifth time in two weeks that I have had to restore you to your comfortable couch. Where have you been this time? "

" Off with Bikey," murmured Jimmieboy, rubbing his eyes and gazing about his nursery.

" Nonsense," said his daddy, the owner of the familiar voice. " With Bikey? Why Bikey has been in the laundry all night." Which fact Bikey never denied, but nowadays when the incident is mentioned he agitates his cyclometer violently, and shakes all over as if he thought it was a good joke on somebody.

In all of which I am inclined to agree with him.

BEFORE HIM STOOD THE IMP.

—See Page 92.

THE IMP OF THE TELEPHONE

I

JIMMIEBOY MAKES HIS AC-QUAINTANCE

THE telephone was ringing, of that there was no doubt, and yet no one went to see what was wanted, which was rather strange. The cook had a great way of rushing up from the kitchen to where the 'phone stood in the back hall whenever she heard its sounding bells, because a great many of her friends were in the habit of communicating with her over the wire, and she didn't like to lose the opportunity to hear all that was going on in the neighborhood. And then, too, Jimmieboy's papa was at work in the library not twenty feet away, and surely one would hardly suppose that

he would let it ring as often as Jimmieboy
had heard it this time—I think there were
as many as six distinct rings—without going
to ask the person at the other end what on
earth he was making all that noise about.
So it was altogether queer that after sounding six times the bell should fail to summon
any one to see what was wanted. Finally
it rang loud and strong for a seventh time,
and, although he wasn't exactly sure about
it, Jimmieboy thought he heard a whisper
repeated over and over again, which said,
" Hullo, Jimmieboy! Jimmieboy, Hullo!
Come to the telephone a moment, for I want
to speak to you."

Whether there really was any such whisper as that or not, Jimmieboy did not delay
an instant in rushing out into the back hall
and climbing upon a chair that stood there
to answer whoever it was that was so anxious to speak to somebody.

"Hullo, you!" he said, as he got his little mouth over the receiver.

"Hullo!" came the whisper he thought he had heard before. "Is that you Jimmieboy?"

"Yes. It's me," returned Jimmieboy. "Who are you?"

"I'm me, too," answered the whisper with a chuckle. "Some people call me Hello Hithere Whoareyou, but my real name is Impy. I am the Imp of the Telephone, and I live up here in this little box right over where your mouth is."

"Dear me!" ejaculated Jimmieboy in pleased surprise. "I didn't know anybody ever lived in that funny little closet, though I had noticed it had a door with a key-hole in it."

"Yes, I can see you now through the key-hole, but you can't see me," said the Imp, "and I'm real sorry you can't, for I am ever so pretty. I have beautiful mauve-colored eyes with eyelashes of pink, long and fine as silk. My eyebrows are sort of green like the lawn gets after a sun shower in the late spring. My hair, which is hardly thicker than the fuzzy down or the downy fuzz—as you prefer it—of a peach, is colored like the lilac, and my clothes are a bright red, and I have a pair of gossamer wings to fly with."

" Isn't there any chance of my ever seeing you? " asked Jimmieboy.

" Why, of course," said the Imp. " Just the best chance in all the world. Do you remember the little key your papa uses to lock his new cigar box with? "

" The little silver key he carries on the end of his watch chain? " queried Jimmieboy eagerly.

" The very same," said the Imp. " That key is the only key in this house that will fit this lock. If you can get it and will open

84

the door you can see me, and if you will eat a small apple I give you when we do meet, you will smallen up until you are big enough to get into my room here and see what a wonderful place it is. Do you think you can get the key?"

"I don't know," Jimmieboy answered. "I've asked papa to let me have it several times already, but he has always said no."

"It looks hopeless, doesn't it?" returned the Imp. "But I'll tell you how I used to do with my dear old father when he wouldn't let me have things I wanted. I'd just ask him the same old question over and over again in thirteen different ways, and if I didn't get a yes in answer to one of 'em, why, I'd know it was useless; but the thirteenth generally brought me the answer I wanted."

"I suppose that would be a good way," said Jimmieboy, "but I really don't see how I could ask for the key in thirteen different ways."

85

"You don't, eh?" said the Imp, in a tone of disappointment. "Well, I *am* surprised. You are the first little boy I have had anything to do with who couldn't ask for a thing, no matter what it was, in thirteen different ways. Why, it's as easy as falling up stairs."

"Tell me a few ways," suggested Jimmie-boy.

"Well, first there is the direct way," returned the Imp. "You say just as plainly as can be, 'Daddy, I want the key to your cigar box.' He will reply, 'No, you are too young to smoke,' and that will make your mamma laugh, which will be a good thing in case your papa is feeling a little cross when you ask him. There is nothing that puts a man in a good humor so quickly as laughing at his jokes. That's way number one," continued the Imp. "You wait five minutes before you try the second way, which is,

86

briefly, to climb upon your father's knee and say, 'There are two ends to your watch chain, aren't there, papa?' He'll say, 'Yes; everything has two ends except circles, which haven't any;' then you laugh, because he may think that's funny, and then you say, 'You have a watch at one end, haven't you?' His answer will be, 'Yes; it has been there fifteen years, and although it has been going all that time it hasn't gone yet.' You must roar with laughter at that, and then ask him what he has at the other end, and he'll say, 'The key to my cigar box,' to which you must immediately reply, 'Give it to me, won't you?' And so you go on, leading up to that key in everything you do or say for the whole day, if it takes that long to ask for it thirteen times. If he doesn't give it to you then, you might as well give up, for you'll never get it. It always worked when I was little, but it may have been be-

cause I put the thirteenth question in rhyme
every time. If I wanted a cream cake, I'd
ask for it and ask for it, and if at the twelfth
time of asking I hadn't got it, I'd put it to
the person I was asking finally this way—

> 'I used to think that you could do
>   Most everything; but now I see
> You can't, for it appears that you
>   Can't give a creamy cake to me.' "

"But I can't write poetry," said Jimmieboy."

"Oh, yes you can!" laughed the Imp.
"Anybody can. I've written lots of it. I
wrote a poem to my papa once which pleased
him very much, though he said he was sorry
I had discovered what he called his secret."

"Have you got it with you?" asked Jimmieboy, very much interested in what the
Imp was saying, because he had often
thought, as he reflected about the world, that
of all the men in it his papa seemed to him

88

to be the very finest, and it was his great
wish to grow up to be as like him as possible; and surely if any little boy could, as
the Imp had said, write some kind of poetry,
he might, after all, follow in the footsteps of
his father, whose every production, Jimmieboy's mamma said, was just as nice as it
could be.

"Yes. I have it here, where I keep everything, in my head. Just glue your ear as
tightly as you can to the 'phone and I'll recite it for you. This is it:

"I've watched you, papa, many a day,
    And think I know you pretty well;
You've been my chum—at work, at play—
    You've taught me how to romp and spell.

"You've taught me how to sing sweet songs;
    You've taught me how to listen, too;
You've taught me rights; you've shown me wrongs;
    You've made me love the good and true.

"Sometimes you've punished me, and I
    Sometimes have wept most grievously
That yours should be the hand whereby
    The things I wished were kept from me.

89

THE IMP OF THE TELEPHONE

"Sometimes I've thought that you were stern;
  Sometimes I could not understand
Why you should make my poor heart burn
  By scoldings and by reprimand.

"Yet as it all comes back, I see
  My sorrows, though indeed most sore
In those dear days they seemed to me,
  Grieved you at heart by far the more.

"The frowns that wrinkled up your brow,
  That grieved your little son erstwhile,
As I reflect upon them now,
  Were always softened by a smile

"That shone, dear father, in your eyes;
  A smile that was but ill concealed,
By which the love that in you lies
  For me, your boy, was e'er revealed."

Here the Imp stopped.

"Go on," said Jimmieboy, softly.

"There isn't any more," replied the Imp.
"When I got that far I couldn't write any
more, because I kind of got running over.
I didn't seem to fit myself exactly. Myself
was too big for myself, and so I had to stop
and sort of settle down again."

"Your papa must have been very much pleased," suggested Jimmieboy.

"Yes, he was," said the Imp; "although I noticed a big tear in his eye when I read it to him; but he gave me a great big hug for the poem, and I was glad I'd written it. But you must run along and get that key, for my time is very short, and if we are to see Magnetville and all the wire country we must be off."

"Perhaps if the rhyme always brings about the answer you want, it would be better for me to ask the question that way first, and not bother him with the other twelve ways," suggested Jimmieboy.

"That's very thoughtful of you," said the Imp. "I think very likely it would be better to do it that way. Just you tiptoe softly up to him and say,

> "If you loved me as I love you,
>   And I were you and you were me,
> What you asked me I'd surely do,
>   And let you have that silver key."

"I think that's just the way," said Jimmieboy, repeating the verse over and over again so as not to forget it. "I'll go to him at once."

And he did go. He tiptoed into the library, at one end of which his papa was sitting writing; he kissed him on his cheek, and whispered the verse softly in his ear.

"Why, certainly," said his papa, when he had finished. "Here it is," taking the key from the end of his chain. "Don't lose it, Jimmieboy."

"No, I'll not lose it. I've got too much use for it to lose it," replied Jimmieboy, gleefully, and then, sliding down from his papa's lap, he ran headlong into the back hall to where the telephone stood, inserted the key in the key-hole of the little door over the receiver and turned it. The door flew open, and before him stood the Imp.

II

IN THE IMP'S ROOM

"DEAR me!" ejaculated Jimmie-boy, as his eye first rested upon the Imp. "That's you, eh?"

"I believe so," replied the Imp, standing on his left leg, and twirling around and around until Jimmieboy got dizzy looking at him. "I was me when I got up this morning, and I haven't heard of any change since. Do I look like what I told you I looked like?"

"Not exactly," said Jimmieboy. "You said you had lilac-colored hair, and it's more like a green than a lilac."

"You are just like everybody else naming your colors. People are very queer about

93

things of that sort, I think.   For instance,"
said the Imp, to illustrate his point, " you
go walking in the garden with one of your
friends, and you come to a rose-bush, and
your friend says, ' Isn't that a pretty rose-
bush ? '   ' Yes,' say you ; ' very.'   Then he
says, ' And what a lovely lilac-bush that is
over there.'   ' Extremely lovely,' say you.
' Let's sit down under this raspberry-bush,'
says he.   Well, now you think lilac is a delicate lavender, rose a pink, and raspberry a
red—eh ? "

"Yes," said Jimmieboy.   "That's the
way they are."

" Well, maybe so ; but that lilac-bush and
rose-bush and raspberry-bush are all the
same color, and that color is green, just like
my hair ; you must have thought I looked
like a rainbow or a paint shop when I told
you about myself ? "

" No," said Jimmieboy.   " I didn't think

94

that, exactly. I thought, perhaps, you were like the pictures in my *Mother Goose* book. They have lots of colors to 'em, and they are not bad looking, either."

" Well, if they are not bad looking," said the Imp, with a pleased smile, " they must be very much like me. But don't you want to come in? "

" I'm not small enough," said Jimmieboy; " but I'll eat that apple you spoke about, and maybe it 'll make me shrink, though I don't see how it can."

" Easy enough. Haven't you seen a boy doubled up after eating an apple? Of course you have; perhaps you were the boy. At any rate there is no reason why, if an apple can work that way, it can't work the other. It's a poor rule that won't work both ways, and an apple is pretty good, as a rule, and so you have it proved without trying that what I say is true. Here's the apple;

eat it as quickly as you can and give me the core."

Jimmieboy took the dainty piece of fruit in his hand and ate it with much relish, for it was a very sweet apple, and he was fond of that sort of thing. Unfortunately, he liked it so well that he forgot to give the core to the Imp, and, when in a moment he felt himself shrinking up, and the Imp asked for the core, he was forced blushingly to confess that he had been very piggish about it, and had swallowed the whole thing.

"I've half a mind not to let you in at all!" cried the Imp, stamping his foot angrily upon the floor, so angrily that the bells rang out softly as if in remonstrance. "In fact, I don't see how I can let you in, because you have disobeyed me about that core."

"I'm surprised at you," returned Jimmieboy, slightly injured in feeling by the Imp's behavior. "I wouldn't make such a fuss about an old apple-core. If you feel as badly about it as all that, I'll run down into the kitchen and get you a whole apple—one as big as you are."

"That isn't the point at all," said the Imp. "I didn't want the core for myself at all. I wanted it for you."

"Well, I've got it," said Jimmieboy, who had now shrunk until he was no taller than the Imp himself, not more than two inches high.

"Of course you have, and if you will notice it is making you grow right back again to the size you were before. That's where the trouble comes in with those trick apples. The outside makes you shrink, and the core makes you grow. When I said I wanted the core I meant that I wanted it to keep until we had had our trip together, so that when we got back you could eat it, and return to

97

your papa and mamma just as you were in the beginning. Just run to the parlor mirror now and watch yourself."

Jimmieboy hastened into the parlor, and climbing upon the mantel-piece gazed into the mirror, and, much to his surprise, noticed that he was growing fast. He was four inches high when he got there, and then as the minutes passed he lengthened inch by inch, until finally he found himself just as he had been before he ate the apple.

"Well, what are you going to do about it?" he asked, when he returned to the telephone.

"I don't know," said the Imp. "It's really too bad, for that's the last apple of that sort I had. The trick-apple trees only bear one apple a year, and I have been saving that one for you ever since last summer, and here, just because you were greedy, it has all gone for nothing."

" I'm very sorry, and very much ashamed," said Jimmieboy, ruefully. " It was really so awfully good, I didn't think."

" Well, it's very thoughtless of you not to think," said the Imp. " I should think you'd feel very small."

" I do!" sobbed Jimmieboy.

" Do you, really?" cried the Imp, gleefully. " Real weeny, teeny small."

" Yes," said Jimmieboy, a tear trickling down his cheek.

" Then it's all right," sang the Imp, dancing a lovely jig to show how glad he felt. " Because we are always the way we feel. If you feel sick, you are sick. If you feel good, you are good, and if you feel sorry, you are sorry, and so, don't you see, if you feel small you are small. The only point is, now, do you feel small enough to get into this room?"

" I think I do," returned Jimmieboy,

brightening up considerably, because his one great desire now was not to be a big grown-up man, like his papa, who could sharpen lead-pencils, and go out of doors in snow-storms, but to visit the Imp in his own quarters. "Yes," he repeated, "I think I do feel small enough to get in there."

"You've got to know," returned the Imp. "The trouble with you, I believe, is that you think in the wrong places. This isn't a matter of thinking; it's a matter of knowing."

"Well, then, I know I'm small enough," said Jimmieboy. "The only thing is, how am I to get up there?"

"I'll fix that," replied the Imp, with a happy smile. "I'll let down the wires, and you can come up on them."

Here he began to unwind two thin green silk-covered wires that Jimmieboy had not before noticed, and which were coiled about two small spools fastened on the back of the door.

"I can't climb," said Jimmieboy, watching the operation with interest.

"Nobody asked you to," returned the Imp. "When these have reached the floor I want you to fasten them to the newel-post of the stairs."

"All right," said Jimmieboy, grasping the wires, and fastening them as he was told. "What now?"

"Now I'll send down the elevator," said the Imp, as he loosened a huge magnet from the wall, and fastening it securely upon the two wires, sent it sliding down to where Jimmieboy stood. "There," he added, as it reached the end of the wire. "Step on that; I'll turn on the electricity, and up you'll come."

"I won't fall, will I?" asked Jimmieboy, timidly.

"That depends on the way you feel," the Imp answered. "If you feel safe, you are safe. Do you feel safe?"

"Not very," said Jimmieboy, as he stepped aboard the magnetic elevator.

"Then we'll have to wait until you do," returned the Imp, impatiently. "It seems to me that a boy who has spent weeks and weeks and weeks jumping off plush sofas onto waxed hard-wood floors ought to be less timid than you are."

"That's true," said Jimmieboy. "I guess I feel safe.

"All aboard, then," said the Imp, pressing a small button at the back of his room.

There was a rattle and a buzz, and then the magnet began to move upward, slowly at first, and then with all the rapidity of the lightning, so that before Jimmieboy had an opportunity to change his mind about his safety he was in the Imp's room, and, much to his delight, discovered that he was small enough to walk about therein without having to stoop, and in every way comfortable.

"At last!" ejaculated the Imp, grasping his hand and giving it an affectionate squeeze. "At last you are here. And now we'll close the door, and I'll show you my treasures."

With this the door was closed, and for a moment all was dark as pitch; but only for a moment, for hardly had Jimmieboy turned around when a flood of soft light burst forth from every corner of the room, and the little visitor saw upon every side of him the most wonderful books, toys, and musical instruments he had ever seen, each and all worked by electricity, and apparently subject to the will of the Imp, who was the genius of the place.

III

ELECTRIC COOKING

"**H**URRAH!" cried Jimmieboy, in ecstasy. "This is great, isn't it?"

"Pretty great," assented the Imp, proudly. "That is, unless you mean large. If you mean it that way it isn't great at all; but if you mean great like me, who, though very, very small, am simply tremendous as a success, I agree with you. I like it here very much. The room is extremely comfortable, and I do everything by electricity—cooking, reading, writing—everything."

"I don't see how," said Jimmieboy.

"Oh, it's simply a matter of buttons and batteries. The battery makes the electricity,

I press the buttons, and there you are. You know what a battery is, don't you?"

"Not exactly," said Jimmieboy. "You might explain it to me."

"Yes, I might if I hadn't a better way," replied the Imp. "I won't explain it to you, because I can have it explained to you in another way entirely, though I won't promise that either of us will understand the explanation. Let's see," he added, rising from his chair and inspecting a huge button-board that hung from the wall at the left of the room. "Where's the Dictionary button? Ah, here—"

"The what?" queried the visitor, his face alive with wonderment.

"The Dictionary button. I press the Dictionary button, and the Dictionary tells me whatever I want to know. Just listen to this."

The Imp pressed a button as he spoke,

and Jimmieboy listened. In an instant there was a loud buzzing sound, and then an invisible something began to speak, or rather to sing:

> " She's my Annie,
> I'm her Joe.
> Little Annie Rooney—"

" Dear me! " cried the Imp, his face flushing to a deep crimson. " Dear me, I got the wrong button. That's my Music-room button. It's right next the Dictionary button, and my finger must have slipped. I'll just turn ' Annie Rooney ' off and try again. Now listen."

Again the Imp touched a button, and Jimmieboy once more heard the buzzing sound, followed by a squeaking voice, which said:

" Battery is a noun—plural, batteries. In baseball the pitcher and catcher is the battery; in electricity a battery is a number of Leyden jars, usually arranged with their inner coatings connected, and their outer coatings also connected, so that they may be all charged and discharged at the same time."

"Understand that, Jimmieboy?" queried the Imp, with a smile, turning the Dictionary button off.

"No, I don't," said Jimmieboy. "But I suppose it is all right."

"Perhaps you'd like an explanation of the explanation?" suggested the Imp.

"If it's one I can understand, I would," returned Jimmieboy. "But I don't see the use of explanations that don't explain."

"They aren't much good," observed the Imp, touching another button. "This will make it clear, I think."

"The Dictionary doesn't say it," said another squeaking voice, in response to the touch of the Imp on the third button; "but a battery is a thing that looks like a row of

107

jars full of preserves, but isn't, and when properly cared for and not allowed to freeze up, it makes electricity, which is a sort of red-hot invisible fluid that pricks your hands when you touch it, and makes them feel as if they were asleep if you keep hold of it for any length of time, and which carries messages over wires, makes horse-cars go without horses, lights a room better than gas, and is so like lightning that no man who has tried both can tell the difference between them."

Here the squeaking voice turned into a buzz again, and then stopped altogether.

"Now do you understand?" asked the Imp, anxiously.

"I think I do," replied Jimmieboy. "A battery is nothing but a lot of big glass jars in which 'lectricity is made, just as pie is made in a tin plate and custard is made in cups."

"Exactly," said the Imp. "But, of course, electricity is a great deal more useful than pie or custard. The best custard in the world wouldn't move a horse-car, and I don't believe anybody ever saw a pie that could light up a room the way this is. It's a pretty wonderful thing, electricity is, but not particularly good eating, and sometimes I don't think it's as good for cooking as the good old-fashioned fire. I've had pie that was too hot, and I've had pie that was too electric, and between the two I think the too-hot pie was the pleasanter, though really nothing can make pie positively unpleasant."

"So I have heard," said Jimmieboy, with an approving nod. "I haven't had any sperience with pie, you know. That and red pepper are two things I am not allowed to eat at dinner."

"You wouldn't like to taste some of my

electric custard, would you?" asked the Imp, his sympathies aroused by Jimmieboy's statement that as yet he and pie were strangers.

"Indeed I would!" cried Jimmieboy, with a gleeful smile. "I'd like it more than anything else!"

"Very well," said the Imp, turning to the button-board, and scratching his head as if perplexed for a moment. "Let's see," he added. "What is custard made of?"

"Custard?" said Jimmieboy, who thought there never could be any question on that point. "It's made of custard. I know, because I eat it all up when I get it, and there's nothing but custard in it from beginning to end."

The Imp smiled. He knew better than that. "You are right partially," he said. "But there aren't custard-mines or custard-trees or custard-wells in the world, so it has to be made of something. I guess I'll ask my cookery-book."

Here he touched a pink button in the left-hand upper corner of the board.

" Milk — sugar — and — egg," came the squeaking voice. " Three-quarters of a pint of milk, two table-spoonfuls of sugar, and one whole egg."

" Don't you flavor it with anything? " asked the Imp, pressing the button a second time.

" If you want to," squeaked the voice. " Vanilla, strawberry, huckleberry, sarsaparilla, or anything else, pust as you want it."

Jimmieboy's mouth watered. A strawberry custard! " Dear me! " he thought. " Wouldn't that be just the dish of dishes to live on all one's days! "

" Two teaspoonfuls of whatever flavor you want will be enough for one cup of custard," said the squeaky voice, lapsing back immediately into the curious buzz.

"Thanks," said the Imp, returning to the table and putting down the receipt on a piece paper.

"You're welcome," said the buzz.

"Now, Jimmieboy, we'll have two cup custards in two minutes," said the Imp. "What flavor will you have?"

"Strawberry cream, please," said Jimmieboy, as if he were ordering soda-water.

"All right. I guess I'll take sarsaparilla," said the Imp, walking to the board again. "Now see me get the eggs."

He pressed a blue button this time. The squeaky voice began to cackle, and in a second two beautiful white eggs appeared on the table. In the same manner the milk, flavoring, and sugar were obtained; only when the Imp signalled for the milk the invisible voice mooed so like a cow that Jim-

mieboy looked anxiously about him, half expecting to see a soft-eyed Jersey enter the
room.

"Now," said the Imp, opening the eggs
into a bowl, and pouring the milk and flavoring and sugar in with them, and mixing
them all up together, "we'll pour this into
that funnel over there, turn on the electricity, and get our custard in a jiffy. Just
watch that small hole at the end of the funnel, and you'll see the custard come out."

"Are the cups inside? Or do we have to
catch the custards in 'em as they come
out?" asked Jimmieboy.

"Oh, my!" cried the Imp. "I'm glad
you spoke of that. I had forgotten the cups.
We've got to put them in with the other
things."

The Imp rushed to the button-board, and
soon had two handsome little cups in response to his summons; and then casting

them into the funnel he turned on the electric current, while Jimmieboy watched carefully for the resulting custards. In two minutes by the clock they appeared below, both at the same time, one a creamy strawberry in hue, and the other brown.

"It's wonderful!" said Jimmieboy, in breathless astonishment. "I wish I had a stove like that in my room."

"It wouldn't be good for you. You'd be using it all day and eating what you got. But how is the custard?"

"Lovely," said Jimmieboy, smacking his lips as he ate the soft creamy sweet. "I could eat a thousand of them."

"I rather doubt it," said the Imp. "But you needn't try to prove it. I don't want to wear out the stove on custard when it has my dinner still to prepare. What do you say to listening to my library a little while? I've got a splendid library in the next room.

It has everything in it that has ever been written, and a great many things that haven't. That's a great thing about this electric-button business. Nothing is impossible for it to do, and if you want to hear a story some man is going to tell next year or next century you can get it just as well as something that was written last year or last century. Come along."

IV

THE LIBRARY

THE Imp opened a small door upon the right of the room, and through it Jimmieboy saw another apartment, the walls of which were lined with books, and as he entered he saw that to each book was attached a small wire, and that at the end of the library was a square piece of snow-white canvas stretched across a small wooden frame.

" Magic lantern? " he queried, as his eye rested upon the canvas.

" Kind of that way," said the Imp, " though not exactly. You see, these books in this room are worked by electricity, like everything else here. You never have to take the books off the shelf. All you have to do is to fasten the wire connected with the book you want to read with the battery, turn on the current, and the book reads itself to you aloud. Then if there are pictures in it, as you come to them they are thrown by means of an electric light upon that canvas."

"Well, if this isn't the most—" began Jimmieboy, but he was soon stopped, for some book or other off in the corner had begun to read itself aloud.

"And it happened," said the book, "that upon that very night the Princess Tollywillikens passed through the wood alone, and on approaching the enchanted tree threw herself down upon the soft grass beside it and wept."

Here the book ceased speaking.

"That's the story of Pixyweevil and Princess Tollywillikens," said the Imp. "You

117

remember it, don't you?—how the wicked
fairy ran away with Pixyweevil, when he
and the Princess were playing in the King's
gardens, and how she had mourned for him
many years, never knowing what had become of him? How the fairy had taken
Pixyweevil and turned him into an oak sap-
ling, which grew as the years passed by to
be the most beautiful tree in the forest?"

"Oh, yes," said Jimmieboy. "I know.
And there was a good fairy who couldn't tell
Princess Tollywillikens where the tree was,
or anything at all about Pixyweevil, but did
remark to the brook that if the Princess
should ever water the roots of that tree with
her tears, the spell would be broken, and
Pixyweevil restored to her—handsomer than
ever, and as brave as a lion."

"That's it," said the Imp. "You've got
it; and how the brook said to the Princess,
'Follow me, and we'll find Pixyweevil,' and

how she followed and followed until she was tired to death, and—"

"Full of despair threw herself down at the foot of that very oak and cried like a baby," continued Jimmieboy, ecstatically, for this was one of his favorite stories.

"Yes, that's all there; and then you remember how it winds up? How the tree shuddered as her tears fell to the ground, and how she thought it was the breeze blowing through the branches that made it shudder?" said the Imp.

"And how the brook laughed at her thinking such a thing!" put in Jimmieboy.

"And how she cried some more, until finally every root of the tree was wet with her tears, and how the tree then gave a fearful shake, and—"

"Turned into Pixyweevil!" roared Jimmieboy. "Yes, I remember that; but I never really understood whether Pixyweevil

ever became King? My book says, ' And so
they were married, and were happy ever
afterwards ; ' but doesn't say that he finally
became a great potteringtate, and ruled over
the people forever."

" I guess you mean potentate, don't you? "
said the Imp, with a laugh—potteringtate
seemed such a funny word.

" I guess so," said Jimmieboy. " Did he
ever become one of those? "

" No, he didn't," said the Imp. " He
couldn't, and live happy ever afterwards, for
Kings don't get much happiness in this
world, you know."

" Why, I thought they did," returned
Jimmieboy, surprised to hear what the Imp
had said. " My idea of a King was that he
was a man who could eat between meals, and
go to the circus whenever he wanted to, and
always had plenty of money to spend, and a
beautiful Queen."

"Oh no," returned the Imp. "It isn't so at all. Kings really have a very hard time. They have to be dressed up all the time in their best clothes, and never get a chance, as you do, for instance, to play in the snow, or in summer in the sand at the seashore. They can eat between meals if they want to, but they can't have the nice things you have. It would never do for a King to like ginger-snaps and cookies, because the people would murmur and say, ' Here—he is not of royal birth, for even we, the common people, eat ginger-snaps and cookies between meals; were he the true King he would call for green peas in wintertime, and boned turkey, and other rich stuffs that cost much money, and are hard to get; he is an impostor; come, let us overthrow him.' That's the hard part of it, you see. He has to eat things that make him ill just to keep the people thinking he is royal and not like them."

"Then what did Pixyweevil become?" asked Jimmieboy.

"A poet," said the Imp. "He became the poet of everyday things, and of course that made him a great poet. He'd write about plain and ordinary good-natured puppy-dogs, and snow-shovels, and other things like that, instead of trying to get the whole moon into a four-line poem, or to describe some mysterious thing that he didn't know much about in a ten-page poem that made it more mysterious than ever, and showed how little he really did know about it."

"I wish I could have heard some of Pixyweevil's poems," said Jimmieboy. "I liked him, and sometimes I like poems."

"Well, sit down there before the fire, and I'll see if we can't find a button to press that will enable you to hear them. They're most of 'em nonsense poems, but as they are perfect nonsense they're good nonsense.

"It is some time since I've used the library," the Imp continued, gazing about him as if in search of some particular object. "For that reason I have forgotten where everything is. However, we can hunt for what we want until we find it. Perhaps this is it," he added, grasping a wire and fastening it to the battery. "I'll turn on the current and let her go."

The crank was turned, and the two little fellows listened very intently, but there came no sound whatever.

"That's very strange," said the Imp. "I don't hear a thing."

"Neither do I," observed Jimmieboy, in a tone of disappointment. "Perhaps the library is out of order, or the battery may be."

"I'll have to take the wire and follow it along until I come to the book it is attached to," said the Imp, stopping the current and

123

loosening the wire. "If the library is out of order it's going to be a very serious matter getting it all right again, because we have all the books in the world here, and that's a good many, you know—more'n a hundred by several millions. Ah! Here is the book this wire worked. Now let's see what was the matter."

In a moment the whole room rang with the Imp's laughter.

"No wonder it wouldn't say anything," he cried. "What do you suppose the book was?"

"I don't know," said Jimmieboy. "What?"

"An old copy-book with nothing in it. That's pretty good!"

At this moment the telephone bell rang, and the Imp had to go see what was wanted.

"Excuse me for a moment, Jimmieboy," he said, as he started to leave the room.

"I've got to send a message for somebody. I'll turn on one of the picture-books, so that while I am gone you will have something to look at."

The Imp then fastened a wire to the battery, turned on the current, and directing Jimmieboy's attention to the sheet of white canvas at the end of the library, left the room.

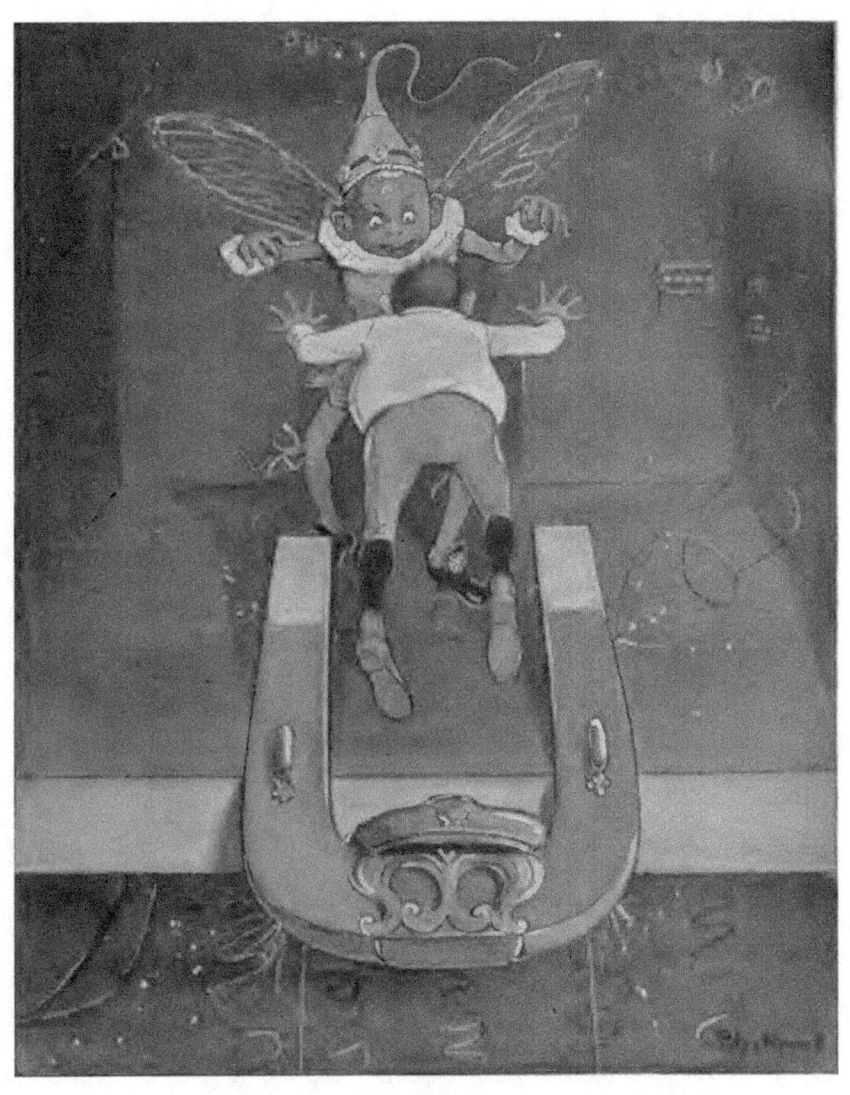

"AT LAST," EJACULATED THE IMP.

—*See Page 103.*

V

THE CIRCUS

THE pictures that now followed one another across the canvas were better than any circus Jimmieboy ever went to, for the reason that they showed a water circus in which were the finest imaginable sea-monsters doing all sorts of marvellous things; and then, too, the book the Imp had turned on evidently had some reading matter in it, for as the pictures passed before the little fellow's eyes he could hear verses describing what was going on, repeating themselves from a shelf directly back of him.

First of all in the circus was the grand parade. A great big gilded band-wagon

126

drawn by gayly caparisoned Sea-Horses
went first, and then Jimmieboy could judge
how much better electric circus books were
than those he had in his nursery, for this
book was able to do what his had never done
—it furnished music to go with the band—
and such music as it was! It had all the
pleasant features of the hand-organ; was as
soft and sweet in parts as the music-box in
the white-and-gold parlor, and once in a
while would play deliciously out of tune like
a real circus band. After the band-wagon
there followed the most amusing things that
Jimmieboy ever saw, the Trick Oysters,
twelve in number, and all on foot. Next
came the mounted Scallops, riding ten
abreast on superbly groomed Turtles, holding the bridle of each of which walked Lob-
sters dressed as Clowns. Then came the
menagerie, with great Sea-Lions swimming
in tanks on wheels; marine Giraffes stand-

ing up to their necks in water forty feet deep; four-legged Whales, like the Oysters, on foot, and hundreds of other queer fish, all doing things Jimmieboy had never supposed they could do.

When the parade was over a great circus ring showed itself upon the canvas, and as strains of lovely music came from the left of the tent the book on the shelf began to recite:

> "The Codfish walks around,
>   The Bass begins to sing;
> The Whitebait 'round the Terrapin's cage
>   Would better get out of the ring.
> The Gudgeon is the fish
>   That goes to all the shows,
> He swims up to the Teredos
>   And tweaks him by the nose."

"That Gudgeon must have been a sort of Van Amberg," thought Jimmieboy. "He did brave things like that."

Then the book went on again:

"The Oyster now will please come forth
And show the people here
Just how he stands upon his head
And then doth disappear."

This interested Jimmieboy very much, and he watched the canvas intently as one of the Trick Oysters walked out into the ring, and after kissing his hand to Jimmieboy and bowing to the rest of the audience —if there were any to bow to, and Jimmieboy supposed there must be, for the Oyster certainly bowed—he stood upon his head, and then without a word vanished from sight.

"Hooray!" shouted Jimmieboy, whereupon the book resumed:

"Now watch the ring intently, for
The Sea-Giraffe now comes,
And without any effort turns
A plum-cake into crumbs."

"Huh!" cried Jimmieboy, as he watched the Sea-Giraffe turn the plum-cake into crumbs. "That isn't anything to do. I could do that myself, and make the plum-cake and the crumbs disappear too."

The book, of course, could not reply to this criticism, and so went right on.

> "The Lobster and the Shark will now
>   Amuse the little folks
> By making here, before their eyes,
>   Some rhymes and funny jokes."

When the book had said this there appeared on the canvas a really handsome Shark clad in a dress suit and a tall hat on his head, followed closely by a Lobster wearing a jester's coat and cap and bells, and bearing in his hand a little stick with Punch's head on the end of it.

"How do you do?" the Lobster seemed to say, as he reached out his claw and grabbed the Shark by his right fin.

"Sir," returned the Shark,

> "If you would really like to know,
>   I'm very glad to say
> That I am feeling pretty fine,
>   And think 'twill snow to-day."

"I'm very glad to see you, Sharkey," said the Lobster. "It is exceedingly pleasant to one who is always joking to meet a Fish like you."

> "I pray excuse me, Lobster dear,
> If I should ask you why?
> Pray come and whisper in my ear,
> What your words signify."

"Certainly, my dear Shark," replied the Lobster. "It is always exceedingly pleasant for a droll person to tell his jokes to a creature with a mouth as large as yours, because your smile is necessarily a tremendous one. I never like to tell my jokes to people with small mouths, because their smiles are limited, while yours is as broad as the boundless ocean."

"Thank you," returned the Shark. "That reminds me of a little song, and as I see you have a bass-drum in your pocket, I will sing it, if you will accompany me."

Here Jimmieboy had the wonderful experience of seeing a Lobster take a bass-drum out of his pocket. I shall not attempt to describe how the lobster did it, because I know you are anxious to hear the Shark's song—as also was Jimmieboy—which went as follows :—that is, the words did ; the tune I cannot here reproduce, but any reader desirous of hearing it can do so if he will purchase a bass-drum set in G-flat, and beat it forty times to the second as hard as he knows how.

> "I find it most convenient to
>   Possess a mouth like this,
> Why, twenty babes at one fell swoop
>   I easily can kiss;
> And sixty pounds of apple pie,
>   Plus ten of orange pulp,
> And forty thousand macaroons
>   I swallow at a gulp.
>
> "It's big enough for me without
>   Appearing like a dunce
> To stand upon a platform and
>   Say forty things at once.

So large it is I have to wear
　　Of teeth a dozen sets,
And I can sing all in a bunch
　　Some twenty-nine duets.

"Once I was captured by some men,
　　Who put me in a lake,
Where sadly I did weep all day—
　　All night I kept awake:
And when the morning came at last,
　　So weary, sir, was I,
I yawned and swallowed up that pond,
　　Which left me high and dry.

"Then when my captors came to me,
　　I opened both my jaws,
And snapped each one of them right up
　　Without a moment's pause;
I swallowed every single man
　　In all that country round,
And as I had the lake inside,
　　They every one were drowned."

Here the Shark stopped, and Jimmieboy applauded.

"And what became of you?" asked the Lobster. "Did you die then?"

133

"Well," returned the Shark, with a puzzled expression on his face. "The song stops there, and I don't know whether I died or not. I presume I did, unless I swallowed myself and got into the lake again in that way. But, see here, Lobby, you haven't got off any jokes for the children yet."

"No, but I'm ready," returned Lobby. "What's the difference between me and Christmas?"

> "Perhaps I'm very stupid,
> Sometimes I'm rather slow—
> But why you're unlike Christmas
> I'm sure I do not know,"

replied the Shark.

"Oh no, you aren't stupid," said the Lobster. "It would be far-stupider of you to guess the answer when it is my turn to make the little ones laugh. The reason I am different from Christmas is just this—now don't lose this, children—with Christmas comes Santa Claus, and with me comes Lobster claws. Now let me give you another. What is it that's brown like a cent, is bigger than a cent, is worth less than a cent, yet costs a cent? "

> "Perhaps I do not know enough
> To spell C-A-T, cat—
> And yet I really must confess
> I cannot answer that,"

returned the Shark.

" I am very glad of that," said the Lobster. " I should have felt very badly if you could, because, you know, I want these children here to observe that while there are some things you can do that I can't do, there are also some things I can do that you can't do. Now the thing that is brown like a cent, is bigger than a cent, is worth less than a cent, yet costs a cent, is a cent's worth of molasses taffy—which the Terrapin will now pass around for sale, along with my photographs, for the benefit of my family."

Then the Lobster bowed, the Shark and he locked fin and arm again, and amid the strains of music from the band marched out of the ring, and Jimmieboy looking up from the canvas for a moment saw that the Imp had returned.

VI

THE CIRCUS CONTINUES

"HULLO," said Jimmieboy. "Back again?"

"Do I look it?" asked the Imp.

"Yes, I think you do," returned Jimmieboy. "Unless you are your twin brother; are you your twin brother?"

"No," laughed the Imp, "I am not. I am myself, and I am back again just as I appear to be, and I've had a real dull time of it since I went away from you."

"Doing what?" asked Jimmieboy.

"Well, first I had to tell your mother that the butcher couldn't send a ten-pound turkey, but had two six-pounders for her if she wanted them; and then I had to tell him for her that he could send mutton instead. After that I had to blow up the grocer for your father, whose cigars hadn't come, and then tell your father what wasn't so—that the cigars hadn't been ordered—for the grocer. After that, just as I was leaving, the cook came to the 'phone and asked me to tell your Aunt Susan's cook that her cousin in New York was very ill with a broken wheel on his truck, and that if she would meet her in town at eleven o'clock they could go to the matinée together, which she said she would do, and altogether it has been a very dull twenty minutes for me. Have you enjoyed yourself?"

"Hugely," said Jimmieboy; "and I hope now that you've come back I haven't got to stop enjoying myself in the same way. I'm right in the middle of the Fish Circus."

"Oh, are you," said the Imp, with a smile.

138

"I rather enjoy that myself. How far have you got?"

"The Shark and the Lobster had just gone off when you came back."

"Good," returned the Imp. "The best part of the performance is yet to come. Move over there in the chair and make room for me. There—that's it. Now let's see what's on next. Oh yes. Here comes the Juggling Clam; he is delightful. I like him better that way than if he was served with tomato ketchup.

The Book interrupted the Imp at this point, and observed:

> "Now glue your eyes upon the ring,
>   And see the Juggling Clam
> Transform a piece of purple string
>   Into a pillow-sham.
>
> "Nor think that when he has done so
>   His tricks are seen and done,
> For next he'll turn a jet-black crow
>   Into a penny bun.

139

" Next from his handsome beaven hat
    He'll take a piece of pie,
A donkey, and a Maltese cat,
    A green bluebottle fly;

" A talking doll, a pair of skates,
    A fine apartment-house,
A pound of sweet imported dates,
    A brace of roasted grouse;

" And should you not be satisfied
    When he has done all that,
He'll take whatever you decide
    Out of that beaver hat.

" And after that he'll lightly spring
    Into the atmosphere,
And show you how a Clam can sing
    If he but persevere.

" When he has all this to you,
    If you applaud him well
He'll be so glad he'll show you through
    His handsome pinky shell."

Jimmieboy didn't believe the Clam could do all this, and he said so to the Imp, but the Imp told him to " wait and see," and when the boy did wait he certainly did see, for the Clam did everything that was promised, and when Jimmieboy, just to test the resources of the wonderful hat, asked the Clam to bring out three dozen jam tarts, the Clam brought out the three dozen jam tarts —only they were picture jam tarts, and Jimmieboy could only decide that it was a wonderful performance, though he would have liked mightily to taste the tarts, and see if they were as good as they looked.

"What comes next?" queried Jimmieboy, as the Clam bowed himself out of the ring.

"Listen, and the Book will tell," returned the Imp.

The Book resumed:

> "We now shall have the privilege
>   Of witnessing the Whale
> Come forth, and set our teeth on edge
>   By standing on his tail.
>
> "When this is done, he'll open wide
>   That wondrous mouth of his,
> And let us see how the inside
>   Of such great creatures is;

"And those who wish to take a trip—
Like Jonah took one time—
Can through his mammoth larynx slip
For one small silver dime.

"For dollars ten, he'll take you to
The coast of Labrador,
The Arctic Ocean he'll go through
For dollars twenty-four;

"And should you wish to see the Pole,
He'll take you safely there,
If you will pay the usual toll—
Ten thousand is the fare."

"I'd like to go to the North Pole," said Jimmieboy.

"Got ten thousand dollars in your pocket?" queried the Imp, with a snicker.

"No; but I've got a dollar in my iron bank," said Jimmieboy; "perhaps he'd take me for that."

"Very likely he would," said the Imp. "These circus fellows will do almost anything for money; but when he got you there he would tell you you could stay there until you paid the other $9999; and think how awful that would be. Why, your ears would be frozen solid inside of four weeks."

"Is it as cold as that at the Pole?" said Jimmieboy.

"Colder!" ejaculated the Imp. "Why, when I was there once I felt chilly in spite of my twenty-eight seal-skin sacques and sixty-seven mufflers, so I decided to build a fire. I got the fagots all ready, lit the match, and what do you suppose happened?"

"What?" queried Jimmieboy, in a whisper, for he was a little awed by the Imp's manner. "Wouldn't the match light?"

"Worse than that," replied the Imp. "It lit, but before I could touch it to the fagots the flame froze!"

Jimmieboy eyed the Imp closely. This seemed to him so like a fairy story, in which the first half is always untrue and the last

143

half imaginary, that he did not exactly know whether the Imp meant him to believe all he said or not. It did him no particular good, though, to scrutinize the Imp's countenance, for that worthy gave not the slightest sign that there was any room for doubt as to the truth of this story; indeed, he continued:

" Why, the last time I went to the North Pole I took forty-seven thermometers to register the coolth of it, and the mercury not only went down to the very bottom of every one of them, but went down so quickly that it burst through the glass bulb that marked 4006 below zero, and fell eight miles more before it even began to slow up. It was so cold that some milk I carried in a bottle was frozen so hard that it didn't thaw out for sixteen months after I got back, although I kept it in boiling water all the time, and one of the Esquimaux who came up there in

144

midsummer to shoot polar bears had to send for a plumber after his return home to thaw out his neck, which had frozen stiff."

"Maybe that is why the Whale charges so much to take people there," suggested Jimmieboy.

"It is, exactly. There is no risk about it for him, but he has to eat so much hot coal and other things to warm him up, that really it costs him nearly as much as he gets to make the trip. I don't believe that he clears more than half a dollar on the whole thing, even when he is crowded," said the Imp.

"Crowded?" echoed Jimmieboy. "What do you mean by that?"

"Crowded? Why, crowded is an English word meaning jamful and two more," said the Imp.

"But crowded with what?" queried Jimmieboy.

"Why, passengers, of course. What did you suppose? Ink bottles?"

"Then he takes more than one passenger at a time," said Jimmieboy.

"Certainly he does. He'll hold twenty-five boys of your size in comfort, thirty-five in discomfort, forty-five in an emergency, and fifty at a pinch," said the Imp. "But see here, we are losing a lot of circus. There goes the Educated Scallop out of the ring now. I'm sorry you missed him, for he is a tender."

"A what?"

"A tender. That is, he is ten times as marvellous as a wonder. Why that Scallop is the finest comic actor you ever saw. His imitation of a party of sharks off manning is simply the most laughable thing I ever saw," said the Imp, enthusiastically.

"I wish I could understand half of what you say," said Jimmieboy, looking wistfully at the Imp. "Because if I did, you know, I might guess the rest."

146

"What is it you don't understand now?" asked the Imp.

"What is a party of sharks off manning?" queried Jimmieboy.

"Did you ever see a man fishing?" questioned the Imp.

"Yes."

"Well, if a man can fish, why shouldn't a fish man? Sharks can catch men just as easily as men can catch sharks, and the Scallop shows how sharks behave when they catch men—that's all."

"I wish I'd seen it; can't you turn back to that page in the book, and have it done all over again?" asked the boy.

"No, I can't," said the Imp. "It's against the rules of the Library. It hurts a book to be turned back, just as much as it hurts your little finger to be turned back, and in nine cases out of ten turning back pages makes them dogeared; and dogs, or anything that even suggests dogs, are not allowed here. Why, if the other Imps who own this Library with me knew that I had even mentioned dogs they would suspend me for a week. But, my dear boy, we really must stop talking. This time we missed the Crab with the iron claw—why, that Crab can crack hickory nuts with that claw when he's half asleep; and when he's wide awake he can hold a cherry stone a hundred miles a minute, and that's holding mighty fast, I can tell you. Let's hear what the Book has to say now."

" Bang! " said the Book.

" Dear me! " cried the Imp. " Did you hear that! "

" Yes," said Jimmieboy. " What does it mean? "

" It means the circus is all over," said the Imp. " That was the shutting of the Book we heard. It's too bad; but there are other things quite as well worth seeing here. I'll tell you what we'll do—I'll find the Pixy-weevil Poetry Book, and turn that on, and while you are listening, I'll see who that is ringing, for I am quite sure the bell rang a minute ago."

THE ELECTRIC CUSTARD.
—See Page 114.

VII

THE POETRY BOOK, AND THE END

THE Imp then arranged the wires so that the Poetry Book could recite itself to Jimmieboy, after which he went back to his office to see who it was that had been ringing the bell.

"My first poem," said a soft silvery voice from the top shelf, towards which Jimmieboy immediately directed his attention— "my first poem is a perfect gem. I have never seen anything anywhere that could by any possibility be finer than it is, unless it be in my new book, which contains millions of better ones. It is called, 'To a Street Lamp,' and goes this way:

"You seem quite plain, old Lamp, to men,
  Yet 'twould be hard to say
What we should do without you when
  Night follows on the day;

"And while your lumination seems
  Much less than that of sun,
I truly think but for your beams
  We would be much undone.

"And who knows, Lamp, but to some wight,
  Too small for me to see,
You are just such a wondrous sight
  As old Sol is to me!

"Isn't that just terribly lovely?" said the soft silvery voice when the poem was completed.

"Yes; but I don't think it's very funny," said Jimmieboy. "I like to laugh, you know, and I couldn't laugh at that."

"Oh!" said the silvery voice, with a slight tinge of disappointment in it. "You want fun do you? Well, how do you like this? I think it is the funniest thing ever written, except others by the same author:

> "There was an old man in New York
> Who thought he'd been changed to a stork;
>   He stood on one limb
>   'Til his eyesight grew dim,
> And used his left foot for a fork."

"That's the kind," said Jimmieboy, enthusiastically. "I could listen to a million of that sort of poems."

"I'd be very glad to tell you a million of them," returned the voice, "but I don't believe there's electricity enough for me to do it under twenty-five minutes, and as we only have five left, I'm going to recite my lines on 'A Sulphur Match.'

> "The flame you make, O Sulphur Match!
>   When your big head I chance to scratch,
>
> "Appears so small most people deem
>   You lilliputian, as you seem.
>
> "And yet the force that in you lies
>   Can light with brilliance all the skies.
>
> "There's strength enough in you to send
>   Great cities burning to their end;
>
> "So that we have a hint in you
>   Of what the smallest thing can do.

" Don't you like that? " queried the voice, anxiously. " I do hope you do, because I am especially proud of that. The word lilliputian is a tremendous word for a poet of my size, and to think that I was able, alone and unassisted, to lift it bodily out of the vocabulary into the poem makes me feel very, very proud of myself, and agree with my mother that I am the greatest poet that ever lived."

" Well, if you want me to, I'll like it," said Jimmieboy, who was in an accommodating mood. " I'll take your word for it that it is a tremendous poem, but if you think of repeating it over again to me, don't do it. Let me have another comic poem."

" All right," said Pixyweevil—for it was he that spoke through the book. " You are very kind to like my poem just to please me. Tell me anything in the world you want a poem about, and I'll let you have the poem."

"Really?" cried Jimmieboy, delighted to meet with so talented a person as Pixyweevil. "Well—let me see—I'd like a poem about my garden rake."

"Certainly. Here it is:

> "I had a little garden rake
>   With seven handsome teeth,
> It followed me o'er fern and brake,
>   O'er meadow-land and heath.
>
> "And though at it I'd often scowl,
>   And treat it far from right,
> My garden rake would never growl,
>   Nor use its teeth to bite."

"Elegant!" ejaculated Jimmieboy. "Say it again."

"Oh no! we haven't time for that. Besides, I've forgotten it. What else shall I recite about?" queried Pixyweevil.

"I don't know; I can't make up my mind," said Jimmieboy.

"Oh dear me! that's awful easy," returned Pixyweevil. "I can do that with my eyes shut. Here she goes:

"Shall I become a lawyer great,
    A captain of a yacht,
A man who deals in real estate,
    A doctor, or a what?
        Ah me! Oh ho!
        I do not know,
    I can't make up my mind.

"I have a penny. Shall I buy
    An apple or a tart?
A bit of toffee or a pie,
    A cat-boat or a cart?
        Ah me! Oh ho!
        I do not know,
    I can't make up my mind."

"Splendid!" cried Jimmieboy.

"That's harder—much harder," said Pixyweevil, "but I'll try. How is this:

"I bought one day, in Winnipeg,
A truly wondrous heavy egg;
And when my homeward course was run
I showed it to my little son.
        'Dear me!' said he,
        When he did see,
            'I think that hen did
                Splen-did-ly!'

155

"I saw a bird—'twas reddish-brown—
One day while in a country town,
Which sang, 'Oh, Johnny, Get Your Gun;'
And when I told my little son,
  In tones of glee
   Said he, 'Dear me!
    I think that wren did
     Splen-did-ly!' "

"That's the best I can do with splendid," said Pixyweevil.

"Well, it's all you can do now, anyhow," came a voice from the doorway, which Jimmieboy immediately recognized as the Imp's; "for Jimmieboy's mamma has just telephoned that she wants him to come home right away."

"It was very nice, Mr. Pixyweevil," said Jimmieboy, as he rose to depart. "And I am very much obliged."

"Thank you," returned Pixyweevil. "You are very polite, and exceedingly truthful. I believe myself that, as that 'Splendid' poem might say, if it had time,

"I've truly ended
Splen-did-ly."

And then Jimmieboy and the Imp passed
out of the library back through the music
and cookery room. The Imp unlocked the
door, and, fixing the wires, sent Jimmieboy
sliding gleefully down to the back hall,
whence he had originally entered the little
telephone closet.

"Hullo!" said his papa. "Where have
you been?"

"Having a good time," said Jimmieboy.

"And what have you done with the key of
my cigar-box?"

"Oh, I forgot," said Jimmieboy. "I left
it in the telephone door."

"What a queer place to leave it," said his
papa. "Let me have it, please, for I want
to smoke."

And Jimmieboy went to get it, and, sure
enough, there it was in the little box, and it

157

unlocked it, too; but when his father came to open the door and look inside, the Imp had disappeared.

CAUGHT IN TOYTOWN

CAUGHT IN TOYTOWN

IT came about in this way. Jimmieboy had been just a wee bit naughty, and in consequence had to sit in the night nursery all alone by himself for a little while. Now, the night nursery was not an altogether attractive place for a small boy to sit in all by himself, because all the toys were kept in the day nursery, and beyond the bureau drawers there was absolutely nothing in the room which could keep a boy busy for more than five minutes. So it happened that at the end of ten minutes Jimmieboy was at his wits' ends to find out what he should do next. At the end of fifteen minutes he was about to announce to a waiting world outside that he'd make an effort to behave himself, and not tease his

161

small brother any more, when his eye caught sight of a singular little crack in one corner of the room. It was the funniest looking crack he ever saw, as it went zig-zagging on its way from floor to ceiling, and then, as he gazed at it it grew even queerer than ever, for it seemed to widen, and then what should appear at the bottom of it but a little iron gate!

"That's the curiousest thing I've seen yet!" said Jimmieboy, crawling on his hands and knees over to the gate and peering through it. Then he suddenly started back, somewhat frightened, for as he looked through the bars a great gruff voice cried out:—

"That's five dollars you owe. Pay up— now. Quick, or the 'bus will go without me."

And then a funny little old man that looked as if he had stepped out of a Brownie book came to the other side of the gate and thrust his hand through the bars in front of Jimmieboy.

" Hear what I said? " the little old man cried out. " Five dollars—hurry up, or the 'bus 'll go without me, and it gets lost every time it does and then there's a fearful row and I'm discharged."

" I haven't got five dollars," said Jimmieboy. " And, besides, if I had I wouldn't give it to you, because I don't owe it to you."

" You don't owe me five dollars? " cried the little old man angrily. " Well, I like that. Then you mean to say you are a view stealer, do you? "

" I don't know what you mean," said Jimmieboy. " I never stole anything."

" Yes you did, too," shrieked the little old man. " You just took a look through these bars, and that look doesn't belong to you. This country belongs to us. You've used

163

our view and now you say you won't pay for it."

"Oh, I see," said Jimmieboy, who began to understand. "You charge for the view —is that it?"

"Yes," said the little old man more quietly. "We have to make a small charge to keep the view in repair, you know. There was a man here last week who spoiled one of our most beautiful bits of scenery. He looked at it so hard that it was simply used up. And another fellow, with two very sharp eyes, bored a hole through another view further along only yesterday. He gave it a quick, piercing, careless glance, and pop!—his left eye went right through it; and that's the reason we have to make people pay. Sightseers do a deal of damage."

"Well, I'm very sorry," said Jimmieboy. "I didn't know there was any charge or I wouldn't have looked."

164

"Then we're square," said the little old man. "I have instructions to collect five dollars or an apology from every one who uses our views until our Wizard has invented some way of enabling people to put back the views they take without meaning to. Won't you come in and look about you and see what an interesting country we have? You can pay for all you see with apologies, since you have no money."

The little old man turned the key on his side of the gate and opened it.

"Thanks ever so much," said Jimmieboy. "I'd like to come in very much indeed," and in he walked.

"What is this place?" he asked, as he gazed about him and observed that all the houses were made of cake and candy, and that all the trees were fashioned like those that came with his toy farm.

"This," said the little old man, clanging

165

the gate and locking it fast, "is Toyland, and you are my prisoner."

"Your what?" cried Jimmieboy, taking instant alarm.

"My prisoner is what I said," retorted the little old man. "I keep a toy shop in Toyland and I'm going to put you in my show window and sell you to the first big toy that wants to buy you for a Christmas present for his little toy at home."

"I d-don't understand," stammered Jimmieboy.

"Well, you will in a minute," said the little old man. "We citizens of Toyland keep Christmas just as much as you people do, only our toys are children just as your toys are toys. You sell us when you can catch us, and we sell you when we catch you —and, what is more, the boy who is kind to his toys in your country finds his toy master in Toyland kind to him. I am told that you

166

are very good to your toys and keep them very carefully, so you needn't be afraid that you will be given to one of our rough toys, who will drag you around by one leg and leave you standing on your head in the closet all night."

" But I don't want to be sold," said Jimmieboy.

" Well, you'd better, then," retorted the little old man, " because if some one doesn't buy you we'll pack you up in a box and send you out to China to the missionaries. Step right in here, please."

Jimmieboy did not wish to obey in the least, but he didn't dare rebel against the commands of his captor, so, with an anxious glance down the street, he started to do as he was told, when a singular sight met his eye. In glancing down the street he had caught sight of the toy-shop window, and what should he see there but his friends

167

Whitty and Billie and Johnnie and sweet little Bettie Perkins who lived across the way, and half a dozen others of his small friends.

"Fine display, eh?" said the little old man. "Great haul of children, eh?" he added. "Best window in town, and they'll sell like hot cakes."

"You've got all my friends except Tommy Hicks," said Jimmieboy.

"I know it," said the little old man. "We had Tommy this morning, too, but a plush rabbit living up on Main street came in and bought him to put in his little toy stocking. I don't envy Tommy much. He used to treat a plush rabbit he had very badly, and the one that bought him seemed to know it, for as he took Tommy out he kept punching him in the stomach and making him cry like a doll, calling 'mam-mah' and 'pah-pah' all the time. He gave me a dol-

168

lar for Tommy, but I'll charge ten for you.
They'll have to pay a good price for Whitty,
too, because there's so much goes with him.
He's got a collection of postage stamps in
one pocket, a muffin ring and a picture book
in another, and the front of his blouse is
stuffed chock full of horse chestnuts and
marbles. Whitty makes a singularly rich
toy, and I think he'll sell as quickly as any
of you."

"How did you capture him?" asked Jimmieboy, who felt better now that he saw that
he was not alone in this strange land. "Did
he come through that crack that I came
by?"

"No, indeed," said the little old man.
"He came in through the pantry door. He
climbed into his mamma's pantry after
some jam, and while he was there I just
turned the pantry around, and when he'd
filled up on jam he walked right through the

169

door into the back of my shop, and before he knew it I had him priced and sitting in the window. There was a wax doll in here this afternoon who wanted to buy him for her daughter Flaxilocks, but she only had $8, and I'm not going to let Whitty go for less than $12, considering all the things he's brought with him."

Then Jimmieboy entered the shop, and it was indeed a curious place. Instead of there being toys on the shelves waiting to be bought, there were piles of children lying there, while the toys were to be seen walking up and down the floor, pricing first a boy and then a baby and then a little girl. The salesmen were all Brownies, and most obliging ones. It didn't seem to be a bit of trouble to them to show goods, and they were very kind to the little toys that had come in with their mothers, punching the children they had to sell in the stomach to make them

170

say what they were made to say; and making them show how easily and gracefully they could walk, and, in short, showing off their wares to the very best advantage. Jimmieboy was too interested in what he saw to feel very anxious, and so, when the bazaar door had closed behind them, he asked the little old man very cheerfully what he should do.

"Step right into the window and sit down," said the little old man. "Smile cheerfully and once in a while get up and twirl around on your right leg. That will attract the attention of the toys passing on the street, and maybe one of 'em will come in and buy you. Do you sing?"

"Yes," said Jimmieboy. "Why?"

"Nothing. I only wanted to know so that I could describe you properly on the placard you are to wear," said the little old man. "How would you like to be called the Automatic-Musical-Jimmieboy?"

"That would be first rate," said Jimmieboy. "Only I couldn't begin to remember it, you know."

"You don't have to," said the little old man. "Nobody will ask you what you are, because the placard will tell that. Only whenever anybody wants to see you, and I take you out of the window, you must sing of your own accord. That's what I mean by calling you an Automatic-Musical-Jimmieboy. It means simply that you are a Jimmieboy that sings of its own accord."

So the placard was made, and Jimmieboy put it on, and got into the window, where, for hours, he was stared at by rag babies, tin soldiers, lead firemen, woolen monkeys and all sorts of other toys, who lived in this strange land, and who were walking in throngs on the sugared sidewalk without. One woolen monkey called in to price him, and Jimmieboy sang a German kindergarten song for him, but the monkey found him too expensive, for, as you may already know, it rarely happens that woolen monkeys have as much as $10 in their pockets.

A little later a wooden Noah, out of an ark across the street, came in, and purchased Whitty, and Jimmieboy began to feel tired and lonesome. The novelty of it all wore off after awhile, and some of the toys in the street bothered him a good deal by making faces at him, and a plaster lion said he thought he'd go in and take a bite of him, he looked so good, which Jimmieboy didn't like at all, though it was meant to be complimentary.

Finally he was sold to a rubber doll with a whistle in its head, and the first thing he knew he was wrapped up in a bundle and put in a pasteboard box to be sent by express to the rubber doll's cousin, who lived in the country. Jimmieboy didn't like this at all,

173

and as the little old man tied the string that fastened him in the box he resisted and began to kick, and he kicked so hard that something fell over with a crash, and, freeing his arms from the twine and the box and the paper, he sprang up and began laying about him with his fists. The little old man fled in terror. The rubber doll changed his mind and said he didn't think he cared for so violent a toy as the Automatic-Musical-Jimmieboy after all, and started off. Jimmieboy, noting the terror that he inspired by his resistance, grabbed up three of the Brownies who were trying to hide in the fire extinguisher, and rushed shouting out of the shop and landed—where do you suppose?

Slap, bang in his own nursery!

How the nursery got there or what became of the Brownies he does not know to this day, but he remembers every detail of

174

his experience very well and it is from him that I got the story. The queerest thing about it, though, is that Whitty has no recollection of the adventure at all, which is really very strange, for Whitty has a marvellous memory. I have known both Whitty and Jimmieboy to remember things that never happened at all, which makes Whitty's loss of memory on this occasion more wonderful than ever.

At any rate, this story tells you exactly what happened to Jimmieboy that day at the beginning of the Christmas vacation, and I am convinced that few of you have ever had anything at all like it happen to you, which is why I have told you all about it.

TOTHERWAYVILLE; THE ANIMAL TOWN

TOTHERWAYVILLE; THE ANIMAL TOWN

"WHAT place is this?" said Jimmieboy, as the express train came to a full stop. "I didn't know fast trains stopped at funny little places like this—and *do* look! Why there is a horse sitting in a wagon driving a pair of men up hill."

"Better not try to know too much about diss yere place, mistah," said the colored porter of the car Jimmieboy was travelling in. "Hit's a powahful funny sort o' place, but hit's just as well fo' you to stay on de kyar an' not go foolin' outside less you's asked."

"I should say it was queer," returned Jimmieboy, "but I can't help feeling that

I'd like to know all about it. What is it called?"

"Totherwayville," returned the porter. "Hit's called like dat because everything in it's done the other way from how you'd do it. If you walked outside on de platform ob de station likely as not some little dog would come up and tie you to a chain an' go leadin' you round town; 'nd you, you couldn't say a woyd. You'd only bark like as though you only was a dog and dey'd give you bones to eat when dey didn't forget it—less dey thought you was a cat, an' den dey'd most likely forget to feed you on milk, de way you does with yo' cat."

"I haven't got any cat," said Jimmieboy.

"Dat's lucky fo' de cat," returned the porter. "Not dat I tinks yo' ain't as good an' kind a little boy as ebber lived, sah, but just because ebbery body dat owns cats sort of don't treat 'em as well as dey'd treat

a baby for instance. De kindest heartedest
little boy in de worl' would forget to gib his
cat its dinner if he had a new toy to play
wid, or a new suit o' party dress to put on to
show his poppy when he come home."

The porter was called away for a minute
by an old lady at the other end of the car
who wanted to know what time the seven
ten train generally started, and while he
was gone Jimmieboy gazed wonderingly out
of the window; and I can't say that I blame
him for doing so, for Totherwayville was indeed a most singular place. There were
very few men, women or children in the
streets and those that were there appeared
to live in a state of captivity. Small dogs
led boys around by a string or a chain; some
of the boys wore muzzles. Here and there
were men tied to hitching posts, and all
about were animals which Jimmieboy had
always hitherto supposed were to be found

181

only in the wild countries, or in circuses and zoological gardens.

Off in a field a hundred or more yards from the station were a lot of monkies playing base-ball, and drollest of all, in front of the Totherwayville hotel, stood a huge lion smoking a cigar and talking with an elephant.

"Well I never!" said Jimmieboy. "This seems to be a regular wild animal place."

Just as he spoke a baby elephant came running down to the station holding a small envelope in his trunk. When he got to the platform he looked anxiously about him and then walking up to a funny looking baboon, who appeared to be depot master, engaged him in earnest conversation. The baboon took the envelope, read the address written upon it and said "he would see."

Then he walked to the end of Jimmieboy's car and called for the porter.

"Well, whad yo' want?" asked the porter.

"Here's an invitation from the mayor to a young man who is said to be on this car," said the baboon. "If he is, will you give it to him?"

"Certainly," said the porter, his face wreathing with smiles. "Certainly. He's hyah."

Jimmieboy watched all this with interest, little thinking that the invitation was for no less a person than himself. He soon discovered the fact, however, for the porter came to him instantly and handed him the envelope. It was addressed simply to:

> MASTER JIMMIEBOY,
> Care of the Porter,
> Express Train, No. 6098.
> Kindness of
> Thomas Baby Elephant.

183

"For me?" cried Jimmieboy.

"Yassir," said the porter. "Hit's for you."

Hurriedly tearing the envelope open, Jimmieboy took from it a delicately scented card on which was engraved:

> The Wild Animals
> Request your presence at their
> wonderful   Exhibition   of
> Trained Hagenbecks,
> This Afternoon at Two
> Absolute Safety Guaranteed.
> R. S. V. P.

"Dear me!" cried Jimmieboy, excitedly, "I couldn't think of going. I should be afraid."

"Oh, you needn't be afraid," said the porter. "Dey'se promised you absolute safety, and I'll tell yo' just one thing. Animals soldom makes promises, but when dey does, dey keeps 'em. Dey's sort ob different from people in dat. Hit's twice as hard to get 'em to make promises but dey seems to be able to keep 'em twice as easy as people. I'd go if I were you. De conductor 'll keep de train waitin' fo' you. Dere's on'y one man aboard dat's in a hurry an' he's travellin' on a free pass, so de road ain't liable fo' any delays to him. I'll go wid you'."

"But how do you know it 'll be safe," added Jimmieboy. "I want to go very much, but——"

"Howdiknow?" said the porter. "Ain't I took little folks to see de show befo? Oh co'se I has an' dey've had de best time in de worl', an' come back cryin' cause dey couldn't stay a week."

"Very well, then," said Jimmieboy, "You can tell the baboon that I'll be very glad to go."

The porter informed the baboon who in turn acquainted the baby elephant with the fact, whereupon the baby elephant took off his hat and bowing politely to Jimmieboy hastened back to the mayor's office with the little boy's reply.

Shortly after the porter returned and said that he had fixed it with the conductor and that the train would wait, and so Jimmieboy and his chestnut colored friend started off. On the way he was gazed at curiously by more wild animals than he had ever seen before, but they were all very respectful to him, many of them bowing politely. Indeed the only incivility he encountered at all was from a rude little boy who was being led around by a handsome St. Bernard dog. The little boy snapped at him as he passed, but he was promptly muzzled by his master, and deprived of the bone he was eating for his luncheon.

After walking along for about five minutes they came to a great circular building, upon the outside of which was a huge sign.

THE TRAINED HAGEN-
BECKS.

MATINEE TO-DAY.

Admission:

Grown Animals.......50 cents.

Cubs, Puppies, etc....4 dollars.

Jimmieboy laughed. "That's funny. They charge less for grown animals than they do for baby animals."

"Not so funny as your plan, mister," said a gruff voice at Jimmieboy's side, very respectfully however.

Jimmieboy looked around to see who it was that spoke and was a little startled at first to see that it was a fine specimen of a tiger that had addressed him.

187

"Don't shrink," said the tiger, seeing that
the little boy was somewhat frightened. "I
won't hurt you. I'm wild, but I'm kind.
Let me show you my smile—you'll see what
a big smile it is, and some day you'll learn
that an animal with a fine open countenance
like mine is when I smile can't be a bad
animal. But to come back to what you think
is a funny scheme. We charge more for
cubs than for grown animals because they
are more trouble. We talked it all over
when we started the show and we found that
there was ten times as much mischief in a
cub or a puppy as there is in a grown up
bear or dog, so we charged more; only as
we don't mind a little mischief we make the
babies pay only eight times as much as the
others. It's simple and very natural, I
think."

"That's true," said Jimmieboy. "It isn't
so odd after all."

188

And then they went inside, where Jimmieboy was received by the mayor, a very handsome lion, and his wife the lioness. All the other animals cheered and the little boy soon came to feel that he was surrounded by friends; strange friends perhaps, but faithful ones. He sat in the front of the mayor's box and watched the cage-enclosed ring in which the Hagenbecks were to perform. A monkey band played several popular tunes in the gallery, after which the performance began.

First a baboon came out and announced a performance by six trained clowns, who he said would crack jokes and turn somersaults and make funny grimaces just as they did in their native lair. The monkey band struck up a tune and in ran the clowns. To Jimmieboy's eyes they were merely plain everyday circus clowns, but the way the baboon made them prance around was wonderful. One of the clowns was a trifle sulky and didn't want to crack his joke, but the baboon kept flicking him with the end of his whip until finally he did crack it, although he might better not have done so for he did it so badly that he spoiled it.

After this a pelican walked out and announced with a proud air that he would now exhibit his flock of trained dudes, who would dance and sing, and wear beautiful clothes and put the heads of their canes in their mouths as intelligently as though they were pelicans and not dudes. Jimmieboy was delighted with them, for after all he was quite like other boys and was accustomed to lavish a great deal of admiration upon such things as chewing gum and dudes. The most interesting feature of the dude exhibition was their chrysanthemum drill. It must have taken the pelican a long time to teach those dudes to pick up their chrysanthemums and place them in their little button-holes with such military precision as they displayed. Everybody applauded this wildly and a great roar of laughter greeted the dudes' acknowledgment of the applause, for the magnificent way in which they took off their silk hats and bowed was truly droll.

"It's hard to believe they are merely human!" said the tiger to Jimmieboy. "Their intelligence is more that of the pelican than of the human kind."

"With a slight mixture of the monkey mind I should say, too," said the elephant. "I'm told these dudes are very imitative."

"The Jumping Billikins!" cried the manager of the exhibition.

"What on earth is a Jumping Billikins?" asked Jimmieboy, who had never heard of an animal of that kind before.

"Wait and see," said the tiger, with a

191

laugh. "Most people call him a nerve centre, but you wouldn't understand that, so I say wait and see."

As Jimmieboy could do nothing else he waited and in a minute the jumping Billikins appeared, followed by six men. The jumping Billikins was nothing more than a pretty little boy, about five years of age, and what he did chiefly was to jump. The six men would put sofas about the ring and the jumping Billikins would jump from one to the other as easily as though he were a real chamois-skin goat. Then he gave a remarkable exhibition of his hopping powers. He hopped up and down on one leg for twenty-eight minutes, much to the wonderment of the elephant, who strong as he was couldn't hop on one leg at all.

"Now watch the men," whispered the tiger. "The jumping Billikins is going to have a romping match with them, and you'd hardly believe it but he'll have them worn out in less than five minutes and yet he'll be as fresh as a rose when he gets through."

Jimmieboy watched, and such a romp as followed he never had seen before. The jumping Billikins was everywhere all the time. One second he'd be riding pickaback on one man, the next you'd find him sitting on another man's head trying to put his feet into the vest pockets of the third and fourth men, while with his hands he'd be playing tag with the others. There was no describing that romp, but as the tiger had said, before five minutes the men were exhausted and the jumping Billikins, fresh as ever, was bowing his thanks to the audience for their applause. Then he walked proudly from the ring and the worn-out men were carried off by the baboon's assistants.

The next thing on the programme was a talking contest between a parrot and a chat-

193

terbox, but this Jimmieboy never saw, for a sudden shriek from the engine waiting with the train at the station for his return called him away. The animals expressed their regret at his early departure and re-quested him to come again sometime, which the little fellow promised to do.

" *I* doan tink yo'll go again, mistah," said the porter, with a smile, as the train drew away from the station.

" Why not? " asked Jimmieboy.

" Because——" said the porter. " Be-cause——"

And then, strange to say, he faded out of sight and Jimmieboy, rubbing his eyes, was astonished to find that he wasn't on a rail-way train at all but in his papa's lap, where he had been all along.

"NO WONDER IT WOULDN'T SAY ANYTHING," HE
CRIED.—*See Page 124.*

AN ELECTRICAL ERROR

AN ELECTRICAL ERROR

JIMMIEBOY'S father and mother had occasion to go to the city for a couple of days recently, and inasmuch as Jimmieboy is such a very movey young person they did not deem it well to leave him at home in the care of the nurse, who had as much as she could do taking care of his brothers, and so they took him along with them. One evening, having to go out to dinner, they invited a young man in Jimmieboy's father's employ to come up to the hotel and stay about and keep the little fellow amused until his bedtime, and to look out for him as well after that time until their return, which Fred was very willing to do since he received $2 reward for his trouble. He said afterward that he earned the two dollars in the first ten minutes playing Waterloo with Jimmieboy, in which pleasing game Jimmieboy was Wellington and Fred was Napoleon, but once a year he didn't mind earning a dollar or two extra in that way.

After the game of Waterloo was over and the Napoleonic Fred had managed to collect the buttons which had been removed from his vest in the first half of the game, the Wellingtonian Jimmieboy decided that he was tired enough to go to bed, and inasmuch as Fred didn't oppose him very hard, to bed he went, and a half hour later both the boys, young and old, were snoring away as though their lives depended on it. It was quite evident that neither of them was as yet sufficiently strong to stand the game of Waterloo for more than an hour—and I don't really wonder at it, for my own experience has led me to believe that even

Bonaparte and Wellington themselves would have been wearied beyond endurance by an hour's play at that diversion, however well they may have stood up under the anxieties of the original battle. In my first game with Jimmieboy I lost five pounds, eight buttons, a necktie, two handfuls of hair and a portion of my temper. So, as I say, I do not wonder that they were exhausted by their efforts and willing to rest after them, though how either of them could sleep with the other snoring as loud as a factory whistle I could never understand.

Fred must have been unusually weary, for, as you will see, he slept more than Jimmieboy did—in fact, it wasn't later than nine o'clock when the latter waked up.

"Say, Fred," he cried.

Fred answered with a deeper snore than ever.

"Fred!" cried Jimmieboy again. "I want a drink of water."

"Puggrrh," snored Fred.

"Stop your growling and ring the telephone for some ice water," said Jimmieboy, and again Fred answered with a snore, and in his sleep muttered something that sounded like "It'll cost you $10 next time," the meaning of which Jimmieboy didn't understand, but which I think had some reference to what it would cost his father to secure Fred as a companion for Jimmieboy on another occasion.

"Guess I'll have to ring it up myself," said Jimmieboy, and with that he jumped out of bed and rushed to that delightful machine which is now to be found in most of the modern hotels, by means of which you can ring up anything you may happen to want, by turning a needle about on a dial until it points to the printed description of the thing you desire and pushing a red button.

"Wonder how they spell ice water," said Jimmieboy. "E-y-e spells I, and s-e spells sss-e-y-e-s-e, ice." But he looked in vain for any such thing on the dial.

"O, well," he said, after searching and searching, "I'll ring up anything, and when the boy comes with it I'll order the ice water."

So he gave the needle an airy twist, pushed the button, and sat down to wait for the boy. Meanwhile he threw a pillow at Fred, who still lay snoring away on the sofa, only now he was puffing like a freight train engine when its wheels slip on an icy railway track.

"Lazybones," snickered Jimmieboy, as the pillow landed on Fred's curly head. But Fred answered never a word, which so exasperated Jimmieboy that he got up with

201

the intention of throwing himself at his sleeping companion, when he heard a queer noise over by the fireplace.

" Hullo, down there, 521. Is that you? " cried somebody.

Jimmieboy stared at the chimney in blank amazement.

" Hurry up below there, 521. Is that you? " came the voice again.

" This room is 521," replied Jimmieboy, realizing all of a sudden that it was no doubt to him that these words were addressed.

" Well, then, look sharp, will you? Turn off the fire—put it out—do something with it. You can't expect me to come down there with the fire burning, can you? I'm not fireproof, you know," returned the voice.

" There isn't any fire here," said Jimmieboy.

" Nonsense," cried the voice. " What's that roaring I hear? "

"Oh — that," Jimmieboy answered. "That's Fred. He's snoring."

"Ah! Then I will come down," came the voice, and in an instant there was a small fall of soot, a rustling in the chimney, and a round-faced, fat-stomached, white-bearded little old gentleman with a twinkling eye, appeared, falling like a football into the grate and bounding like a tennis ball out into the middle of the floor.

"Santa Claus, at your service," he said, bowing low to Jimmieboy.

The boy looked at him breathless with astonishment for a moment.

"Well—well——" put in the old man impatiently. "What is it you want with me? I'm very busy, so pray don't detain me. Is it one of my new Conversational Brownies you are after? If so, say so. Fine things, these Conversational Brownies."

"I never heard of 'em," said Jimmieboy.

"Coz why?" laughed Santa Claus, twirling airily about on the toes of his left foot. "Coz why? Bee-coz there ain't never been any for you to hear about. I invented 'em all by myself. You have Brownies in books that don't move. Good. I like 'em, you like 'em, we all like 'em. You have Brownies out of books. Better—but they can't talk and all bee-coz they're stuffed with cotton. It isn't their fault. It's the cotton's fault. Take a man and stuff him with cotton and he wouldn't be able to say a word, but stuff him with wit and anecdotes and he'll talk. Wherefore I have invented a Conversational Brownie. He's made of calico, but he's stuffed with remarks, and he has a little metal hole in his mouth, and when you squeeze him remarks oozes out between his lips and there you are. Eh? Fine?"

"Bully," said Jimmieboy.

"Was that what you rang for? Quick, hurry up, I haven't any time to waste at this season of the year."

"Well, no," Jimmieboy answered. "Not having ever heard of 'em, of course."

"Oh, then you wanted one of my live wood doll babies," said Santa Claus. "Of course. They're rather better than the Conversational Brownies, perhaps, I guess; I don't know. Still, they last longer, as long as you water 'em. Was it one of those you wanted?"

"What is a live wood doll baby?" asked Jimmieboy.

"One o' my newest new, new things," replied Santa Claus. "'Stead o' making wooden dolls out of dead wood, I makes 'em out o' live wood. Keep some o' the roots alive, make your doll, plant it proper, water it, and it'll grow just like a man. My live oak dolls that I'm making this year, a

205

hundred years from now will be great giants."

"Splendid idea," said Jimmieboy. "But how about the leaves. Don't they sprout out and hide the doll?"

"Of course they do, if you don't see that they're pulled off," retorted Santa Claus. "You don't expect me to give you toys and look after 'em all at the same time, do you?"

"No," said Jimmieboy.

"Well, it's good you don't," said Santa Claus, turning a somersault backward. It's werry good you don't, for should you had have you'd have been disappointed. But, I say, was that what you wanted, or were you after one of my new patent typewriters that you wind up? Don't keep me waiting all night——"

"I never heard of your new patent typewriters that you wind up," Jimmieboy answered.

"That isn't the question interrupted Santa Claus nervously, "though I suppose it's the answer, for if you had heard of my windable writer it would have been the thing you wanted. It's a grand invention, that machine. You take a key, wind the thing up, having first loaded it with paper, and what do you suppose it does?"

"Writes?" asked Jimmieboy.

"Exactly," replied Santa Claus. "It writes stories and poems and jokes. There are five keys goes with each machine—one poetry key, one joke key, one fairy tale key, a story of adventure key, and a solemn Sunday school story key that writes morals and makes you wonder whether you're as good as you ought to be."

"Well," said Jimmieboy, "now that I know about that, that's what I want, though as a matter of fact I rang you up for a glass of ice water."

207

"What!" cried Santa Claus, indignantly, bounding about the room like a tennis ball again. "Me? Do you mean to say you've summoned me away from my work at this season of the year just to bring you a glass of ice water?"

"I—I didn't mean for you to bring it," said Jimmieboy, meekly. "I—I must have made a mistake——"

"It's outrageous," said Santa Claus, stamping his foot. "You hadn't oughter make mistakes. I won't bring you anything on Christmas—no, not a thing. You——"

A knock at the door interrupted the little old man, and Jimmieboy, on going to see who was there, discovered the hall boy with the pitcher of water.

"What's that?" asked Santa, as Jimmieboy returned.

"It's the water," replied the little fellow. "So I couldn't have made a mistake after all."

"Hum!" said Santa, stroking his beard slowly and thoughtfully. "I guess—I guess the wires must be crossed—so it wasn't your fault—and I will bring you something, but the man who ought to have looked after those wires and didn't won't find anything in his stocking but a big hole in the toe on Christmas.

The old fellow then shook hands good-by with the boy, and walked to the chimney.

"Let's see—what shall I bring you?" he asked, pausing.

"The windable writer," said Jimmieboy.

"All right," returned Santa, starting up the chimney. "You can have one if I get it finished in time, but I am afraid this annoying delay will compel me to put off the distribution of those machines until some other year."

And with that he was gone.

Meanwhile Jimmieboy is anxiously waiting for Christmas to see if it will bring him the windable writer. I don't myself believe that it will, for the last I heard Santa had not returned to his workshop, but whether he got stuck in the hotel chimney or not nobody seems to know.

IN THE BROWNIES' HOUSE

IN THE BROWNIES' HOUSE

JIMMIEBOY, like every other right-minded youth, was a great admirer of the Brownies. They never paid any attention to him, but went about their business in the books as solemnly as ever no matter what jokes he might crack at their expense. Nor did it seem to make any difference to them how much noise was being made in the nursery, they swam, threw snowballs, climbed trees, floated over Niagara, and built houses as unconcernedly as ever. Nevertheless Jimmieboy liked them. He didn't need to have any attention paid to him by the little folk in pictures. He didn't expect it, and so it made no difference to him whatever whether they noticed him or not.

The other day, however, just before the Christmas vacation had come to an end Jimmieboy had a very queer experience with his little picture book acquaintances. He was feeling a trifle lonesome. His brothers had gone to a party which was given by one of the neighbors for the babies, and Jimmieboy at the last moment had decided that he would not go. He wasn't a baby any more, but a small man. He had pockets in his trousers and wore suspenders exactly like his father's, only smaller, and of course a proper regard for his own dignity would not permit him to take part in a mere baby party.

"I'll spend my afternoon reading," he said in a lordly way. "I don't feel like playing 'Here We Go Round the Mulberry Bush' now that I wear suspenders."

So he went down into his father's library where his mother had put a book-case **for**

214

him, on the shelves of which he kept his treasured books. They were the most beautiful fairy books you ever saw; Brownie books and true story books by the dozen; books of funny poetry illustrated by still funnier pictures, and, what I fancy he liked best of all, a half dozen or more big blank books that his father had given him, in which Jimmieboy wrote poems of his own in great capital letters, some of which stood on their heads and others on their sides, but all of which anybody who could read at all could make out at the rate of one letter every ten minutes. I never read much of Jimmieboy's poetry myself and so cannot say how good it was, but his father told me that the boy never had the slightest difficulty in making Massachusetts rhyme with Potato, or Jacksonville with Lemonade, so that I presume they were remarkable in their way.

Arrived in the library Jimmieboy seated

himself before his book-case, and after gloating over his possessions for a few moments, selected one of the Brownie books, curled himself up in a comfortable arm-chair before the fire, and opened the book.

" Why ! " he cried as his eye fell upon one of the picture pages. " That's funny. I never saw that picture before. There isn't a Brownie in it; nothing but an empty house and a yard in front of it. Where can the Brownies have gone? "

He hadn't long to wait for an answer. He had hardly spoken when the little door of the house opened and the Dude Brownie poked his head out and said softly:

> " 'Tis not an empty house, my dear.
> The Brownies all have come in here.
> We've played so long to make you smile
> We thought we'd like to rest awhile.
> We're every one of us in bed
> With night-caps on each little head,
> And if you'll list you'll hear the roar
> With which the sleeping Brownies snore."

216

Jimmieboy raised the book to his ear and listened, and sure enough, there came a most extraordinary noise out of the windows of the house. It sounded like a carpenter at work with a saw in a menagerie full of roaring lions.

"Well, that is funny," said Jimmieboy as he listened. "I never knew before that Brownies ever got tired. I thought they simply played and played and played all the time."

The Dude Brownie laughed.

> "Now there, my boy, is where you make
> A really elegant mistake,"

he said, and then he added,

> "If you will open wide the book
> We'll let you come inside and look.
> No other boy has e'er done that.
> Come in and never mind your hat."

"I wouldn't wear my hat in the house anyhow," said Jimmieboy. "But I say,

Mr. Brownie, I don't see how I can get in there. I'm too big."

> "Your statement makes me fancy that
> You really don't know where you're at;
> For, though you're big and tall and wide,
> Already, sir, you've come inside,"

replied the Dude Brownie, and Jimmieboy, rubbing his eyes as if he couldn't believe it, looked about him and discovered that even as the Dude Brownie had said, he had without knowing it already accepted the invitation and stood in the hall of the Brownie mansion. And O! such a mansion! It was just such a house as you would expect Brownies to have. There were no stairs in it, though it was three stories high. On the walls were all sorts of funny pictures, pictures of the most remarkable animals in the world or out of it, in fact most of the pictures were of animals that Jimmieboy had never heard of before, or even imagined. There was the

Brownie Elephant, for instance, the cunningest little animal you ever saw, with forty pairs of spectacles running all the way down its trunk; and a Brownie Pugdog with its tail curled so tightly that it lifted the little creature's hind legs off the floor; and most interesting of all, a Brownie Bear that could take its fur off in hot weather and put on a light flannel robe instead. Jimmieboy gazed with eyes and mouth wide open at these pictures.

"What queer animals," he said. "Do you really have such animals as those?"

"Excuse me," said the Dude Brownie anxiously, "but before I answer, must I answer in poetry or in prose? I'll do whichever you wish me to, but I'm a little tired this afternoon, and poetry is such an effort!"

"I'm very fond of poetry," said Jimmieboy, "especially your kind, but if you are tired and would rather speak the other way, you can."

The Dude Brownie smiled gratefully.

" You're a very kind little man," he said. " This time I'll talk the other way, but some day when I get it written I'll send you my book of poetry to make up for it. You like our animals, do you? "

" Very much," said Jimmieboy. " I'd like to see a Brownie zoo some time."

" I'll attend to that," said the Dude Brownie. " I'll make a note of it on the wall so that we won't forget it."

Here he seized a huge pencil, almost as big as himself, and wrote something on the wall which Jimmieboy could not read, but which he supposed was the Brownie's memorandum.

" Won't you spoil your wall doing that? " queried the little visitor.

" Oh no," said the Brownie. " All these

walls are made of slate and we use 'em to write on. It saves littering the house all up with paper, and every Tuesday we have a house-cleaning bee and rub all the writing off. It's a very good scheme and I wonder your grown-up people don't have it, particularly in your nurseries. I've noticed children writing things on nursery walls lots of times and then they've been scolded for doing it because their nurses said it spoiled the paper. I can't understand why they don't have slate walls instead that can't be spoiled. It's such a temptation to write on a wall, but it does spoil paper. But to come back to our animals, they're really lovely, and have such wonderfully sweet dispositions. There is the Brownie Elephant, for instance—he's the most light hearted creature you ever saw, and he has holes bored through his trunk like a flute and at night he plays the most beautiful music on

221

it, while we Brownies sit around and listen to him."

"What does he wear so many pairs of spectacles for?" asked Jimmieboy.

"He has weak eyes," said the Brownie. "That is, he has at night. He can't see his notes to play tunes by when it is dark, and so we've provided him with those spectacles to help him out. Then the Bear is very self-sacrificing. If anyone of us wants to go out anywhere in the cold he'll let us have his robe just for the asking. The Pug-dog isn't much use but he's playful and intelligent. If you tell him to go to the post-office for your mail he'll rush out of the front door, down the road to the grocer's and bring you back an apple or an orange, because he always knows that there isn't any mail. One of your hired men wouldn't know that, but would waste his time going to the post-office to find it out if you told him to."

Jimmieboy expressed his admiration of the intelligence of the Brownie Dog and the good nature of the other animals, and then asked if he mightn't go upstairs he was so curious to see the rest of the house.

"Certainly," said the Dude Brownie, "only you'll have to slide up the banisters. We haven't any stairs."

"Don't think I know how," said Jimmieboy. "I can slide down banisters, but I never learned to slide up 'em."

"You don't have to learn it," returned the Brownie. "All you have to do is to get aboard and slide. It's a poor banister that won't work both ways. The trouble with your banisters is that they are poor ones. Climb aboard and let yourself go."

The boy did as he was told, and pop! the first thing he knew he was in the midst of the Brownies on the second floor. Much to his surprise, while they were unquestionably snoring, they were all reading, or writing, or engaged in some other occupation.

"Well this beats everything!" said Jimmieboy. "I thought you said they were asleep?"

"They are," said the Dude Brownie. "So am I, for that matter, but we don't waste our time just because we happen to be asleep. Some of us do our best work while we are resting. The Chinese Brownie washes all our clothes while he's asleep, and the Dutch Brownie does his practising on his cornet at the same time. If people like you did the same thing you'd get twice as much work done. It's all very well and very necessary too to get eight hours of sleep every day, but what's the use of wasting that time? Take your sleep, but don't loaf while you're taking it. When I was only a boy Brownie I used to play all day and go to school after I'd gone to bed. In that way I learned a great deal and never got tired of school. You don't get tired while you are asleep."

"It's a wonderful plan," said Jimmieboy, "and I wish I knew how to work it. I'm not very fond of school myself and I'd a great deal rather play than go there in the daytime. Can't you tell me how it's done so that I can tell my papa all about it? Maybe he'd let me do it that way if I asked him."

"Of course I'll tell you," said the Dude Brownie. "It's just this way. You go to bed, pull the covers up over you, shut your eyes, fall asleep, and then—"

Alas! The sentence was never finished, for as the Brownie spoke a gong in the hall-way below began to clang fearfully, and in an instant the whole Brownie troupe sprang to the banisters, slid down into the hall and rushed out into the yard. Their play time

225

had come, and their manager had summoned them back to it. Jimmieboy followed, but he slid so fast that it made him dizzy. He thought he would never stop. Down the banisters he slid, out through the hall to the yard, over the heads of the Brownies he whizzed and landed with a thud in the soft embrace of the armchair once more, and just in time too, for hardly had he realized where he was when in walked his father and mother, and following in their train were his two baby brothers, their mouths and hands full of sweetmeats.

"Hullo," said Jimmieboy's father. "Where have you been, Jimmieboy?"

"In the Brown——" began the boy, but he stopped short. It seemed to him as if the Dude Brownie in the book tipped him a wink to be silent, and he returned the wink.

"I've been here, looking at my Brownie book," he said.

" Indeed? " said his father. " And do you never get tired of it? "

" No," said Jimmieboy quietly, " it seems to me I see something new in it every time I open it," and then in spite of the Brownie's wink he climbed out of the chair into his papa's lap and told him all that occurred, and his papa said it was truly wonderful, especially that part which told about how much could be done by an intelligent creature when fast asleep.

"I'M VERY GLAD TO SEE YOU, SHARKEY," SAID
THE LOBSTER.——*See Page 131.*

JIMMIEBOY — and SOMETHING

JIMMIEBOY—and SOMETHING

I T was a warm, summer afternoon—just
the sort of an afternoon for a drowse,
and when the weather was just right
for it Jimmieboy was a great drowser. In
fact, a little golden-haired fairy with a
silver wand had just whispered to a butter-
fly that when it came to drowsing in an interesting way there was nobody in the world
who could excel Jimmieboy in that accom-
plishment. Jimmieboy had overheard this
much himself, but he had never told anybody about it, because he found drowsing
so very easy, and the pleasures of it so great,
that he was a little afraid somebody else
might try it and make him divide up his fun
with him. It was somewhat selfish of him
to behave this way, perhaps, but then no one

231

ever pretended that Jimmieboy was absolutely perfect, not even the boy himself.

It so happened, that upon this particular afternoon, Jimmieboy was swinging idly in the hammock under the trees. On one side of him babbled a little mountain stream, while on the other lay a garden full of beautiful flowers, where the bees hummed the whole day through, and whence when day was done and the night shadows were coming over all even the sun's rays seemed sorry to go. In the house, a hundred feet away, Jimmieboy's mamma was playing softly on a zithern, and the music, floating out through the flower-scented air, set the boy to thinking, which with him is always the preliminary to a doze. His right eye struggled hard to keep awake, long after the left eye had given up the fight, and it was due possibly to this that Jimmieboy was wide enough awake at the time to hear a quaint

little voice up in the tree calling to the tiger
lilies over near the house.

"Say, Tige," the little voice cried,
"what time is it?"

"I can't see the clock," returned the lily.
"But," it added, dropping into verse:

> "I judge from sundry tinkles
> Of the bell upon the cow
> That if it isn't later,
> It is pretty nearly now."

"Thank you," said the voice up the tree,
"I was afraid I'd miss my train."

"So! You are going away?" said another voice, which, if his ears did not de-
ceive Jimmieboy, came this time from the
rose bush.

"Yes," said the voice up in the tree.
"Yes, I'm going away. I don't know where
exactly, because I haven't bought my ticket
yet. I may be going to the North Pole, or I
may only be coming here. In fact, if my

ticket turns out to be a return ticket, it will amount to that, which makes me wonder what's the use of going any way."

"But when does your train go?" asked the voice in the rose bush.

"A week from next Thursday," said the tree voice. "I didn't know but that it was then now. You see I always get mixed up as to what time it is or what day it is. This isn't a date tree, and I haven't any calendar."

"I guess you've got plenty of time," chuckled the tiger lily, nodding its head gleefully at the holly-hock. "It won't be a week from next Thursday for several days yet."

"Heigho," sighed the voice up in the tree. "Several days to wait, eh? I'm sure I don't know what I shall do to pass the time away."

"Oh, as for that," observed the holly-hock; "I know an easy scheme for passing time. I learned it from a fairy I met once.

> " 'Sit still and never raise your hands,'
>   Advised the little elf,
> ' Pay no attention to the clock,
>   And time will pass itself.'

"You have nothing to do with it doing it that way," the holly-hock added.

"That's a good idea," said the voice up in the tree. "It's queer I never thought of it, and I've been thinking and thinking ever so many years, trying to get up a scheme to pass the time."

"You're not very deep, I'm afraid," said the rose bush. "You can't think very valuable thoughts, can you?"

"I'm sure I don't know," the voice up the tree replied. "I've never tried to sell them, so of course I can't tell whether they are valuable or not. Do you sell what you think?"

235

"Certainly I do," returned the rose bush. "I suggested the idea of making honey to the bees. Wasn't that a great thing to do?"

"Yes, indeed," returned the voice. "It was splendid. I've never had any honey, but I'm told it's fine. It's very sticky, isn't it?"

"Very," said the rose bush. "I guess honey is about as sticky as anything can be."

"And very useful for that reason," said the voice up in the tree, kindly. "Very useful. I suppose, really, if it wasn't for honey, people couldn't make postage stamps stay on letters. You ought to be very happy to think that one of your thoughts has given people the idea of mucilage. Do they ever use honey for anything else but its stickiness?"

"Hoh!" jeered the rose bush. "Don't you know anything?"

"Not much," said the tree voice. "I

know you, and me, and several other things, but that's not much, is it? It's really queer how little I know. Why, would you believe it, a sparrow asked me the other day what was the difference between a robin's egg and a red blackberry, and I didn't know."

"What did you tell him?" asked the holly-hock.

"I told him I couldn't tell until I had eaten them."

"And what did he say?" put in the tiger lily, with a grin.

"He said that wasn't the answer; that one was blue and the other was green, but how a red blackberry can be green I can't see," replied the voice up in the tree.

Jimmieboy smiled quietly at this, and the voice up the tree continued:

"Then he asked me what color blueberries were, and I told him they were blue; then he said he'd bet a mosquito I couldn't

237

tell him what color huckleberries were, and
when I said they were of a delicate huckle
he laughed, and said I owed him a mosquito.
I may owe him a mosquito, but I haven't an
idea what he was laughing at."

"That's easy," said the holly-hock. "He
was laughing because there isn't any such
color as huckle."

"I don't think that's funny, though,"
said the voice in the tree. "Indeed, I think
it's sad, because it seems to me that a very
pretty color could be made out of huckle.
Why do you suppose there isn't any such
color?"

The lily and the rose and holly-hock
bushes were silent for a moment, and then
they said they didn't know.

"I'm glad you don't," said the tree voice.
"I'm glad to find that there are some things
you don't know. Just think how dreadful
it would be if you knew everything. Why,

238

if you knew everything, nobody could tell you anything, and then there'd never be any news in the world, and when you heard a joke you couldn't ever laugh because you'd have known it before."

Here Jimmieboy, impressed by the real good sense of this remark, leaned out of the hammock and peered up into the tree to see if possible who or what it was that was speaking.

" Don't," cried the voice. " Don't try to see me, Jimmieboy, I haven't got my company clothes on, and you make me nervous."

" But I want to see who you are," said Jimmieboy.

" Well you needn't want that any more," said the voice. " I'll tell you why. Nobody knows what I am. I don't even know myself."

" But what do you look like? " asked Jimmieboy.

239

"I don't know that, either. I never saw myself," replied the voice. "I'm something, of course, but just what I don't know. It may be that I am a horse and wagon, only I don't think I am, because horses and wagons don't get up in trees. I saw a horse sitting on a whiffletree once, but that was down on the ground and not up here, so, of course, you see the chances are that I'm not that."

"What do you think you are?" asked Jimmieboy.

"I haven't thought much about it. But I'll tell you what I'll do. I'll tell you what, perhaps, I am, and maybe that will help you to find out, and if you do find out I beg that you will tell me, because I've some curiosity on the subject myself."

"Go ahead," said Jimmieboy. "You give me the perhapses and I'll try to guess."

"Well," began the voice, slowly, as if,

whatever it was, the thing was trying to think.   Let me see.

> " Perhaps I am a house and lot,
>   Perhaps I am a pussy cat,
>   Perhaps I am a schooner yacht,
>   Or possibly an inky spot,
>   Perhaps a beaver hat."

" I've never seen any of those up a tree," said Jimmieboy. " I guess you aren't any of those."

" Very likely not," said the voice, " but I can try a few more.

> " Perhaps I am a picture book,
>   It maybe I'm a candy box,
>   Perhaps I am a trolling hook,
>   A tennis bat, or fancy cook,
>   Perhaps a pair of socks.

> " Perchance I am a pair of shears,
>   Perhaps a piece of kindling wood,
>   Perhaps I am a herd of deers,
>   Perhaps two crystal chandeliers,
>   Or some old lady's hood.

241

"No man can say I'm not a pad
  On which a poet scribbles verse,
It may be I'm a nice fresh shad,
Or something else not quite as bad,
  Or maybe something worse."

"But none of these things ever go up trees," protested Jimmieboy. "Can't you tell me some of the things that perhaps you are that are found up in trees?"

"No," said the voice, sadly. "I can't. I don't know what kind of things go up trees —unless it's pollywogs or Noah's arks."

"They don't go up trees," said Jimmieboy, scornfully.

"Well I was afraid they didn't, and that's why I didn't mention them before. But you see," the voice added with a mournful little tremor, "you see how useless it is to try to guess what I am. Why, if you really guessed, I wouldn't know if you'd guessed right—so what's the use?"

"I guess there isn't any use," said Jim-

242

mieboy. "If I could only see you once, though, maybe I could tell."

Here he leaned far out of the hammock, in a vain effort to see the creature he was talking to. He leaned so far out, in fact, that he lost his balance and fell head over heels on to the soft green turf.

The mountain brook seemed to laugh at this mishap, and went babbling on to the great river that bore its waters to the sea, while Jimmieboy, somewhat dazed by his afternoon's experience, walked wonderingly back to the house to make ready for supper. He was filled with regret that he had not been able to catch a glimpse of the strange little being in the tree, for he very much wished to know what manner of creature it was, so stupid and yet so kindly—as, indeed, would I, for really I haven't any more idea as to who or what it was than he. What do *you* think it was?

243

JIMMIEBOY'S FIREWORKS

JIMMIEBOY'S FIREWORKS

IT was a very great misfortune indeed that Jimmieboy should make the acquaintance of the bumblebee at that particular time—that is to say, everybody thought it was. The bumblebee, as a rule, was one of the jolliest bees in the hive, and passed most of his days humming away as if he were the happiest of mortals; but at the particular moment when Jimmieboy, who wasn't looking where he was going, ran into him, the bee was mad about something, and he settled down on Jimmieboy's cheek and stung him. He was a very thorough bee, too, unhappily, and he never did anything by halves, which is why it was that the sting was about as bad a one and as painful as any bee ever stang. I use the word

247

"stang" here to please Jimmieboy, by the way. It is one of his favorites in describing the incident.

Now, it is bad enough, I have found, to be stung by a bee at any time, but when it happens on the night of July Fourth, and is so painful that the person stung has to go to bed with a poultice over his cheek and eye, and so cannot see the fireworks he has been looking forward to for weeks and weeks, it is about the worst affliction that a small boy can have overtake him—at least it seems so at the time—and that was exactly poor Jimmieboy's case. He had thought and thought and thought about those fireworks for days and days and days, and here, on Fourth of July night, he found himself lying in bed in his room, with one side of his face covered with a bandage, and his poor little other blue eye gazing at the ceiling, while his ears listened to the sizzling of the rock-

ets and pinwheels and the thunderous boom-
ing of the bombs.

"Mean old bee!" he said, drowsily, as his
other blue eye tried to peer out of the window in the hope of seeing at least one rocket
burst into stars. "I didn't mean to upset
him."

"I know you didn't," sobbed a little voice
at his side. "And I didn't mean to sting
you, only I didn't know it was you, and I
was mad because somebody's picked a rose
I'd had my eye on for a week, and you ran
into me and spilled all the honey I'd gug—
gathered, and then I—I was so irritated I
stuck my stingers out and stang you. Can't
you forgive me?"

Jimmieboy withdrew his other blue eye
from the window in wonderment. He was
used to queer things, but this seemed the
queerest yet. The idea of a bumblebee coming to apologize to a boy for stinging him

249

made him smile in spite of his disappointment and his pain.

"Who are you?" he said, looking toward the foot of the bed, whence the voice had come.

"I used to be a bumblebee," sobbed the little voice, "but I've changed my first letter from 'b' to 'h.' I'm only an humble-bee now, and all because I've treated you so badly. I really didn't mean to, and I've come to help you have a good time to-night, so that you won't miss the fireworks because of my misbehavior."

"Don't mention it," said Jimmieboy, kindly. "It was my fault, after all. I hadn't ought to have run into you."

"Yes, you had ought to have, too," moaned the little bee. "You were just right in running into me. I hadn't ought to have got in your way."

"Well, anyhow, it's all right," said Jimmieboy. " You're forgiven—though you did hurt me like everything."

" I know it," sobbed the bee. " I almost wish you'd get a pin and stick it into me once, so as to sort of just even things up. It would hurt me, I know, but then I'd feel better after I got well."

" Indeed I won't," said Jimmieboy, with a determined shake of his head. " That won't do any good, and what's the use anyhow, as long as you didn't mean it? "

" I'm sure I don't know," the bee answered. " I'm only a bug, after all, you know, and so I don't understand things that human beings which has got brains can understand. I've noticed, though, that sometimes when a boy gets hurt it sort of makes him feel better if he hurts back."

" I wouldn't mind a bit if I could see the fireworks," said Jimmieboy. " That's what hurts the most."

"Well, I'll tell you what you do," said the bee; "if that's all you feel bad about, we can fix it up in a jiffy. Do you know what a jiffy is?"

"No, I don't," said Jimmieboy.

"Well, I'll tell you," said the bee, "but don't you ever tell:

"Sixty seconds make a minute,
   Sixty minutes make an hour;
But a second has within it
   Sixty jiffies full of power.

In other words, a jiffy is just the same thing to a second as the second is to the minute or the minute to the hour; and, dear me, what billions of things can happen in a jiffy! Why, they're simply enormous."

"They must be," said Jimmieboy, "if, as you say, you can fix me up in regard to the fireworks in a jiffy."

"There isn't any if about it," returned the bee. "Just turn over and put your face into the pillow, and see what you can see."

252

"I can't see anything with both eyes in my pillow, much less with one," said Jimmieboy.

"Well—try it," said the bee. "I know what I'm buzzing about."

So Jimmieboy, just to oblige his strange little friend, turned over and buried his face in the pillow. At first, as far as he could see, there was nothing going on in the pillow to make it worth while; but all of a sudden, just as he was about to withdraw his face, a great golden pinwheel began to whizz and whirr right in front of him, only instead of putting forth fire it spouted jewels and flowers, and finally right out of the middle of it there popped a tiny bit of a creature all dressed in spangles, looking for all the world like a Brownie. He bowed to Jimmieboy politely and requested him to open his mouth as wide as he could.

"What for?" asked Jimmieboy, naturally a little curious to know the meaning of this strange proceeding.

"I am going to set off the sugar-plum bomb," the little creature replied. "But of course if you don't want the sugar-plums you can keep your mouth closed."

"Can't I catch 'em in my hands?" said Jimmieboy.

"You can if you want to, but they won't be of any use if you do," returned the little creature. "You see, this bomb shoots out candy instead of sparks, but the candy is so delicate that, like the sparks in fire fireworks, it goes out just as soon as it comes down. If you catch 'em in your hands you won't be able to see how good they taste, don't you see?"

"Yeh," said Jimmieboy, opening his mouth as wide as he could, and so speaking with difficulty. "Hire ahay!"—by which I presume he meant fire away, only he couldn't say it plainly with his mouth open.

And then the little creature set off the sugar-plum bomb, and the candies it put forth were marvelous in number and sweetness, and, strange to say, there wasn't one of them that, in falling, came down anywhere but in the mouth of the small boy who had been " stang."

" Got any cannon crackers? " asked Jimmieboy, delighted with what he had already seen, as soon as the sweet taste from the sugar-plums died away. " I'm fond of noise, too."

" Well," said the little creature, " we have great big crackers, only they don't break the silence in just the way you mean. They make a noise, but it isn't just a plain ordinary crash such as your cannon crackers make. We call 'em our Grand Opera Crackers. I'll set one off and let you see what I mean."

So the little creature opened a big chest that in some way happened to come up out

of the ground beside him, and with difficulty hauled from it a huge thing that
looked like the ordinary giant crackers that
Jimmieboy was used to seeing. It was twice
as big as the little creature, but he got it
out nevertheless.

"My!" cried Jimmieboy. "That's fine.
That ought to make lots of noise."

"It will," returned the little creature,
touching a match to the fuse. "Just listen
now."

The fuse burned slowly along, and then,
with a great puff of smoke, the cracker
burst, but not into a mere crash as the little
creature had hinted, but into a most en-
trancing military march, that was inspiring
enough to set even the four legs of the
heaviest dinner-table to strutting about the
room. Jimmieboy could hardly keep his
own feet still as the music went on, but he
did not dare draw his face away from the

256

pillow so that he might march about the room, for fear that by so doing he would lose what might remain of this wonderful exhibition, whose like he had never even dreamed of before, and alongside of which he felt that the display he had missed by having to go to bed must be as insignificant as a pin compared to Cleopatra's great stone needle.

"That was fine!" he cried, ecstatically, as the last echoes of the musical cracker died away. "I wouldn't mind having a hundred packs of those. Have you got any music torpedoes?"

"No," returned the little creature. "But we've got picture torpedoes. Look at this." The little creature here took a small paper ball from the chest, and, slamming it on the ground with all his might, it exploded, and the spot whereon it fell was covered with a gorgeous little picture of Jimmieboy him-

self, all dressed in sailor's clothes and dancing a hornpipe.

"That's a very good picture of you," said
the little creature, looking at the dancing
figure. "It's so full of motion, like you.
Here's another one," he added, as the picture from the first torpedo faded away.
"This shows how you'd look if you were a
fairy."

The second torpedo was slammed down
upon the ground just as the first had been,
and Jimmieboy had the pleasure of seeing
himself in another picture, only this time he
had gossamer wings and a little wand, and
he was flying about a great field of poppies
and laughing with a lot of other fairies,
among whom he recognized his little
brothers and a few of his playmates. He
could have looked at this all night and not
grown weary of it, but, like a great many
other good things, the picture could not last

forever, and just at the most interesting point, when he saw himself about to fly a race across the poppy-field with a robin, the picture faded away, and the little creature called out: "Now for the finest of the lot. Here goes the Fairy-Book Rocket!"

With a tremendous whizz, up soared the most magnificent rocket you ever saw. It left behind it a trail of golden fire that was dazzling, and then, when it reached its highest point in the sky, it burst as all other rockets do, but, instead of putting forth stars, all the people in Jimmieboy's favorite fairy tales jumped out into the heavens. There was a glittering Jack chasing a dozen silver giants around about the moon; there was a dainty little Cinderella, with her gorgeous coach and four, driving up and down the Milky Way; Puss-in-Boots was hopping about from one cloud to another, as easily as if he were an ordinary cat jump-

259

ing from an ordinary footstool on to an ordinary sofa. They were all there cutting up
the finest pranks imaginable, when suddenly
Jack of the beanstalk fame appeared at the
side of the little creature who had set the
rocket off, and planted a bean at his feet,
and from it there immediately sprang forth
a huge stalk covered with leaves of gold and
silver, dropping showers of rubies and
pearls and diamonds to the ground, as it
grew rapidly upwards to where the fairy-
land folk were disporting themselves in the
skies. These, when the stalk had reached
its full growth, rushed toward it, and in a
moment were clambering back to earth
again, and then, when they were all safely
down, they ranged themselves in a row,
sang a beautiful good-night song to the boy
with his face in the pillow, and disappeared
into the darkness.

"There!" said the little voice back of

Jimmieboy. "That's what one jiffy will do."

Jimmieboy turned about and smiled happily at the bee—for it was the bee who had spoken.

"Sometime we'll have another," the bee added. "But now I must go—I've got to get ready for to-morrow, which will be bright and sunshiny, and in every way a great day for honey. Good-by!"

And Jimmieboy, as the bee flew out of the window, was pleased to notice that the pain in his cheek was all gone. With a contented smile on his face he turned over and went to sleep, and when his papa came in to look at him as he lay there in his little bed, noticing the smile, he turned to his mamma and said, "Well, he doesn't look as if he'd missed the fireworks very much, after all, does he?"

"No," said his mamma. "He seems to be

261

just the same happy little fellow he always was."

And between us, I think they were both right, for we know that he didn't miss the fireworks, and as for being happy, he was just as much so as are most boys who know what it is to be contented, and who, when trials come upon them, endeavor to make the best of them, anyhow.

"YOUR EARS WOULD BE FROZEN SOLID."

—*See Page 143.*

HIGH JINKS IN THE BARN

HIGH JINKS IN THE BARN

IT was unquestionably a hot day; so hot, indeed, that John, the hired man, said the thermometer had had to climb a tree to get high enough to record the degree of the heat. Jimmieboy had been playing out under the apple-trees for two or three hours, and now, "just for greens," as the saying went, he had climbed into the old barouche in the barn, where it was tolerably cool and there was a soft cushion to lie off on. He closed his eyes for a moment, and then a strange thing happened.

The Wheelbarrow over by the barn door unmistakably spoke. "Say," it said to the Farm Wagon, "there's one thing I like about you."

"What's that?" said the Wagon.

265

"You have such a long tongue, and yet you never say an unkind word about anybody," replied the Barrow, with a creak of its wheel that sounded very much like a laugh.

"That may be so," said the big gray Horse that was used with the fat old bay to pull the farm wagon. "It may be just as you say, but that tongue has come between me and one of my best friends many a time, I tell you."

"I couldn't help that," retorted the Wagon. "The hired man made me do it; besides, I have a grudge against you."

"What's the grudge?" queried the Horse.

"You kicked me and my friend the Whiffletree that day you ran away down in the hay field," replied the Wagon. "I was dreadfully upset that day."

"I should say you were," put in the Rake.

266

"And when you were upset you fell on me and knocked out five of my teeth. I never had such a time."

"You needed to have something done to those teeth, anyhow," said the Sickle. "They were nearly all gone when that happened."

"Oh, were they?" retorted the Rake. "And why were they nearly all gone? Do you know that?"

"I do not. I suppose you had been trying to crack chestnuts with them. Was that it?"

"No, it wasn't," retorted the Rake. "They were worn out cleaning up the lawns after you pretended to have finished them off."

"You think you're bright, don't you?" replied the Sickle, with a sneer.

"Well, if I was as dull as you are," returned the Rake, angrily, "I'd visit the

267

Grindstone and get him to put a little more edge on me."

"Come, come; don't be so quarrelsome," said the Hose. "If you don't stop, I'll drown the whole lot of you."

"Tut!" retorted the Rake. "You look for all the world like a snake."

"He is a snake," put in the Curry-comb. "He's a water-snake. Aren't you, Hosey?"

"I'd show you whether I am or not if the faucet hadn't run dry."

"Dear me!" laughed the Sled. "Hear Hosey talk! The idea of a faucet running! It hasn't moved an inch since it came here. Why, I've got two runners that 'll beat it out of sight on the side of a hill."

"Yes, the down side," said the Pony. "Anything can run down hill. Even a stupid old millstone can do that. But when it comes to running up hill, I'm ahead of you all. Why, the biggest river or ava-

268

lanche in the world couldn't run up hill beside me."

"That's so," put in the Riding-Whip.
"And you and I know who makes you do
it—eh?"

"I didn't say anything about that," said
the Pony. "But I'll tell you one thing: if
you'll come down here where I can reach
you with one of my hind legs, I'll show you
what nice shoes I wear."

"Much obliged," said the Whip. "I
don't wear shoes myself, and am not interested in the subject. But if any man who
is interested in bugs wants to know how to
make a horse fly, I can show him."

"You are a whipper-snapper," said the
Pony angrily.

"Ho! ho!" jeered the Whip.

"Anybody call me?" queried the Hoe,
from the corner where he had been asleep
while all this conversation was going on.

269

Then they all burst out laughing, and peace was restored.

"They say the Fence is worn out," put in the Sickle.

"I should think it would be," replied the Rake. "It's been running all around this place night and day without ever stopping for the last twenty years."

"How many miles is that?" queried the Wagon.

"Well, once around is half a mile, but if it has gone around every night and every day for twenty years," said the Grindstone, "that's one mile every twenty-four hours— 365 miles a year—3,650 miles in ten years, and 7,300 miles in twenty years. Quite a record, eh?"

"That's a good way for a Picket-fence to go," said the Wheelbarrow. "It would kill me to go half that distance."

"Well, if you live until you do go half

that distance," put in the Hose, "you'll never die."

"Ho! ho!" jeered the Barrow.

"Somebody did call me that time!" cried the Hoe, waking up again. "I'm sure I heard my name."

"Yes, you did," said the Rake. "We waked you up to tell you that breakfast would be ready in about a month, and to say that if you wanted any you'd do well to go down to the river and see if you can't buy its mouth, because if you don't, nobody knows how you can eat it."

Here the loud and prolonged laugh caused Jimmieboy once more to open his eyes, and as his papa was standing by the side of the carriage holding out his hands to help him down and take him into the house to supper, the little fellow left the quarrelsome tools and horses and other things to themselves.

271

JIMMIEBOY'S VALENTINE

JIMMIEBOY'S VALENTINE

JIMMIEBOY had been watching for the postman all day and he was getting just a little tired of it. It was Valentine's Day, and he was very naturally expecting that some of his many friends would remember that fact and send him a valentine. Still the postman, strange to say, didn't come.

" He'll be later than usual," said Jimmieboy's mamma. " The postman always is late on Valentine's Day. He has so many valentines to leave at people's houses."

" Well, I wish he'd hurry," said Jimmieboy, " because I want to see what my valentimes look like."

Jimmieboy always called valentines val-

275

entimes, so nobody paid any attention to that mistake—and then the front door bell rang.

"I guess, maybe, perhaps that's the postman—though I didn't hear his whistle," said Jimmieboy, rushing to the head of the stairs and listening intently, but no one went to the door and Jimmieboy became so impatient that he fairly tumbled down the stairs to open it himself.

"Howdy do," he said, as he opened the door, and then he stopped short in amazement. There was no one there and yet his salutation was returned.

"Howdy do!" something said. "I'm glad you came to the door, because I mightn't have got in if the maid had opened it. People who don't understand queer things don't understand me, and I rather think if the girl had opened that door and had been spoken to by something she

276

couldn't see she'd have started to run and hide, shrieking Lawk, meanwhile."

"I've half a mind to shriek Lawk, myself," said Jimmieboy, a little fearfully, for he wasn't quite easy about this invisible something he was talking to. "Who are you, anyhow?"

"I'm not a who, I'm a what," said the queer thing. "I'm not a person, I'm a thing —just a plain, homely, queer thing. I couldn't hurt a fly, so there's no reason why you should cry Lawk."

"Well, what kind of a queer thing are you?" asked Jimmieboy. "Are you the kind of a queer thing I can invite into the house or would it be better for me to shut the door and make you stay outside."

"I don't like to say," said the queer thing, with a pathetic little sigh. "I think I'm very nice and that anybody ought to be glad to have me in the house, but that's only

277

my opinion of myself. Somebody else
might think differently. In fact somebody
else has thought differently. You know
rhinoceroses and crocodiles think themselves very handsome, and that's why they
sit and gaze at themselves in the water all
the time. Everybody else though knows
that they are very ugly. Now that's the way
with me. As I have said, I'm sure in my own
mind that I am perfectly splendid, and
yet your Uncle Periwinkle, who thought of
me, wouldn't write me and send me to you."

"You must be very wise if you know
what you mean," said Jimmieboy. "I
don't."

"Oh, no—I'm not so wise—I'm only
splendid, that's all," said the other. "You
see I'm a valentine, only I never was made.
I was only thought of. Your Uncle Periwinkle thought of me and was going to send
me to you and then he changed his mind

278

and thought you'd rather have a box of candy; so he didn't write me and sent you a box of chocolate creams instead. The postman's got 'em and if he doesn't find out what they are and eat 'm all up you'll receive them this afternoon. Won't you let me come in and tell you about myself and see if you don't like me? I want to be liked—oh ever so much, and I was awfully disappointed when your uncle decided not to send me. I cried for eight minutes and then resolved to come here myself and see if after all he wasn't wrong. Let me come in and if you don't like me I'll go right out again and never come back."

"I like you already, without knowing what kind of a valentime you are," said Jimmieboy, kindly. "Of course you can come in, and you can stay as long as you want to. I don't believe you'll be in anybody's way."

"Thank you very much," said the valen-

279

tine, gratefully, as it moved into the house, and, to judge from where its voice next came, settled down on the big sofa cushion. "I hoped you'd say that."

"What kind of a valentime are you?" asked Jimmieboy in a moment. "Are you a funny one or a solemn one, with paper frills all over it in a box and a little cupid peeping out from behind a tree?"

"I am almost afraid to tell you," said the valentine, timidly. "I am so afraid you won't like me."

"Oh, yes I will," said Jimmieboy, hastily. "I like all kinds of valentimes."

"Well, that's a relief," said the other "I'm comic."

"Hooray!" cried Jimmieboy, "I just love comic valentimes with red and blue pictures in 'em and funny verses."

"Do you really?" returned the valentine, cheerfully. "Then I can say hooray, too,

280

because that's what I was to be. I was to be
a picture of a boy with red trousers on, sitting crosswise on a great yellow broomstick,
galloping through a blue sky, toward a pink
moon. How do you like that?"

"It *is* splendid, just as you said," returned Jimmieboy, with a broad smile.
"Those are my favorite colors."

"You like those colors better than you
do chocolate cream color?" asked the valentine.

"Oh, my yes," said Jimmieboy. "Probably you wouldn't be so good to eat as a
chocolate cream, but for a valentime, you're
much better. I don't want to eat valentimes, I want to keep 'em."

"You don't know how glad you make
me," said the pathetic little valentine, its
voice trembling with happiness. "Now, if
you like my verses as well as you do my picture, I will be perfectly content."

281

"I guess I'll like 'em," said Jimmieboy. "Can you recite yourself to me?"

"I'm not written—didn't I tell you?" returned the valentine. "That's the good part of it. I can tell you what I might have been and you can take your choice."

"That's good," said Jimmieboy. "Then I'm sure to be satisfied."

"Just so," said the valentine. "Now let me think what I might have been! Hum! Well, what do you think of this:

If I had a cat with a bright red tail,
  And a parrot whose voice was soft and low
I'd put 'em away in a water pail,
  And send 'em to where the glowworm's glow.

And then I would sit on an old whisk broom
  And sail through the great, soft starlit sky,
To where the bright moonbeams gaily froom
  Their songs to the parboiled Gemini.

And I'd say to the frooming moonbeams that,
  I'd come from the home of the sweet woodbine,
Deserting my parrot and red-tailed cat,
  To ask if they'd be my valentine."

"I guess that's good," said Jimmieboy. "Only I don't know what frooming is."

"Neither do I," said the valentine, "but that needn't make any difference. You see, it's a nonsense rhyme any how, and I couldn't remember any word that rhymed with broom. Froom isn't a bad word, and inasmuch as it's new to us we can make it mean anything we want to."

"That's true," said Jimmieboy. "But why do you send the cat and the parrot off?"

"They aren't in the picture," said the valentine, "and so of course we have to get rid of them before we have the boy start off on the broomstick. It would be very awkward to go sailing off through the sky on a broomstick with a parrot and cat in tow. Then to show the moonbeams how much the boy thinks of them you have to have him leave something behind that he thinks a great deal of, and that something might just as well be a parrot and a cat as anything else."

"And what does it all mean?" asked Jimmieboy. "Is the boy supposed to be me?"

"No," explained the valentine. "The boy is supposed to be Uncle Periwinkle, and you are the moonbeams. In putting the poem the way I've told you it's just another and nonsense way of saying that he'll be your valentine and will take a great deal of trouble and make sacrifices to do it if necessary."

"I see," said Jimmieboy. "And I think it very nice indeed—though I might like some other verse better."

"Of course you might," said the valentine. "That's the way with everything. No matter how fine a thing may be, there may be something else that might be better, and

284

the thing to do always is to look about and try to find that better thing. How's this:

> " 'The broom went around to Jimmieboy's,
>   And cried, ' Oh, Jimmieboy B.,
>   Come forth in the night, desert your toys,
>   And take a fine ride with me.

> " 'I'll take you off through the starlit sky,
>   We'll visit the moon so fine,
>   If you will come with alacrity,
>   And be my valentine.' "

" That isn't so bad, either," said Jimmieboy. " I sort of wish a broomstick would come after me that way and take me sailing off to the moon. I'd be its valentime in a minute if it would do that. I'd like to take a trip through all the stars and see why they twinkle and——"

" Why they twinkle? " interrupted the valentine. " Why they twinkle? Hoh! Why, I can tell you that—for as a secret just between you and me, *I* know a broomstick that has been up to the stars and he told me all about them. The stars twinkle because from where they are, they are so high up, they can see all that is going on in the world, and they see so many amusing things that it keeps 'em laughing all the time and they have to twinkle just as your eyes do when they see anything funny."

"That's it, is it?" said Jimmieboy.

"Yes, *sir!*" said the valentine, "and it's fine, too, to watch 'em when you are feeling sad. You know how it is when you're feeling sort of unhappy and somebody comes along who feels just the other way, who laughs and sings, how you get to feel better yourself right off? Well, remember the stars when you don't feel good. How they're always twinkling—watch 'em, and by and by you'll begin to twinkle yourself. You can't help it—and further, Jimmieboy," added this altogether strange valentine, "When anybody tries to make you think

286

that this world has got more bad things than good things in it, look at the stars again. They wouldn't twinkle if that was so and until the stars stop twinkling and begin to frown, don't you ever think badly of the world."

"I won't" said Jimmieboy. "I always did like the world. As long as I've been in it I've thought it was a pretty fine place."

"It is," said the valentine. "Nobody can spoil it either—unless you do it yourself—but, I say, if you'd like to have me I'll introduce you to my broomstick friend sometime and maybe some day he'll give you that ride."

"Will you?" cried Jimmieboy with delight. "That will be fine. You are the dearest old valentime that ever was."

Saying which, forgetting in his happiness that the valentine was not to be seen and so could not be touched, Jimmieboy leaned

287

over to hug him affectionately as he sat on the sofa cushion.

Which may account for the fact that when Jimmieboy's papa came home he found Jimmieboy clasping the sofa cushion in his arms, asleep and unconscious of the fact that the postman had come and gone, leaving behind him six comic valentines, four "solemn ones," and a package of chocolate creams from Uncle Periwinkle.

When he waked he was rejoiced to find them, but he has often told me since that the finest valentine he ever got was the one Uncle Periwinkle thought he wouldn't like as well as the candy; and I believe he still has hopes that the invisible valentine may turn up again some day, bringing with him his friend the broomstick who will take Jimmieboy off for a visit to the twinkling stars.

288

THE MAGIC SLED

THE MAGIC SLED

WHEN Jimmieboy waked up the other morning the ground was white with snow and his heart was rejoiced. Like many another small youth Jimmieboy has very little use for green winters. He likes them white. Somehow or other they do not seem like winters if they haven't plenty of snow and he had been much afraid that the season was going to pass away without bringing to him an opportunity to use the beautiful sled Santa Claus had brought him at Christmas.

It was a fine sled, one of the finest he had ever seen. It had a red back, yellow runners and two swan heads standing erect in front of it to tell it which way it should go. On the red surface of the back was painted its name in very artistic blue letters, and that name was nothing more nor less than " Magic."

" Hooray," he cried as he rushed to the window and saw the dazzling silver coating on the lawn and street. " Snow at last! Now I can see if Magic can slide."

He dressed hastily—so hastily in fact that he had to undress again, because it was discovered by his mother, who came to see how he was getting along, that he had put on his stocking wrong side out, and that his left shoe was making his right foot uncomfortable.

" Don't be in such a hurry," said his Mamma. " There was a man once who was always in such a hurry that he forgot to take his head down town with him one day, and when lunch time came he hadn't anything with him to eat his lunch with."

" But I want to slide," said Jimmieboy,

"and I'm afraid there'll be a slaw come along and melt the snow."

Jimmieboy always called thaws slaws, so his mother wasn't surprised at this remark, and in a few minutes the boy was ready to coast.

"Come along, Magic!" he said, gleefully catching up the rope. "We'll see now if Uncle Periwinkle was right when he said he didn't think you'd go more'n a mile a minute, unless you had a roller-skate on both your runners."

And then, though Jimmieboy did not notice it, the left-hand swan-head winked its eye at the other swan-head and whispered, "Humph! It's plain Uncle Periwinkle doesn't know that we are a magic sled."

"Well, why should he?" returned the other swan-head, with a laugh. "He never slode on us."

"I'm glad I'm not an uncle," said the

293

left-hand head. " Uncles don't know half as much as we do."

" And why should they!" put in the other. " They haven't had the importunities we have for gaining knowledge. A man who has lived all his days in one country and which has never slad around the world like us has, don't see things the way us would."

And still Jimmieboy did not notice that the swan-heads were talking together, though I can hardly blame him for that, because, now that he was out of doors he had to keep his eyes wide open to keep from bumping his head into the snow balls the hired man was throwing at him. In a few minutes, however, he did notice the peculiar fact and he was so surprised that he sat plump down on the red back of the sled and was off for—well, where the sled took him, and of all the slides that ever were slid, that was indeed the strangest. No sooner had he sat down than with a leap that nearly threw him off his balance, the swans started. The steel runners crackled merrily over the snow, and the wind itself was soon left behind.

"C-can you sus-swans tut-talk?" Jimmie-boy cried, in amazement, as soon as he could get his breath.

"Oh, no, of course not," said the right-hand swan. "*We* can't talk, can we Swanny?"

"No, indeed, Swayny," returned the other with a laugh. "You may think we talk, you may even hear words from our lips, we might even recite a poem, but that wouldn't be talk—oh, no, indeed. Certainly not."

"It's a queer question for him to ask, eh Swanny?" said the right-hand head.

"Extraordinary, Swayny," said the one

on the left. " Might as well ask a locomotive if it smokes."

" Well, I only wanted to know," said Jimmieboy.

" He only wanted to know, Swanny," said Swayny.

" I presume that was why he asked—as though we didn't know that," said Swanny. " He'd ask a pie-man with a tray full of pies, if he had any pies, I believe."

" Yes, or a cat if he could miaou. Queer boy," returned Swayny. And then he added :

> "I think a boy, who'd waste his time
> In asking questions such as that,
> Would ask a man, who dealt in rhyme
> If he'd a head inside his hat."

Jimmieboy laughed.

" You know poetry, don't you," he said.

" Well, rather," said Swayny. " That is to say, I can tell it from a church steeple."

" Which reminds me," put in Swanny, as

strange to say, this wonderful sled began to slide up a very steep hill, " of a conundrum I never heard before. What's the difference between writing poetry the way some people do and building a steeple as all people do? "

" I can't say," said Swayny, " though if you'll tell me the answer now next time you ask that conundrum I'll be able to inform you."

" Some people who write poetry run it into the ground," said Swanny, " and all people who build steeples, run 'em up into the air."

" That's not bad," said Jimmieboy, with a smile.

"No," said Swanny, " it is not—but you don't know why."

" I don't indeed," observed Jimmieboy. " Why? "

" Because my conundrums never are," said Swanny.

"Europe!" cried Swayny. "*Five minutes for refreshments.*"

"What *do* you mean?" said Jimmieboy, as the sled came to a standstill.

"What does any conductor mean when he calls out the name of a station?" said Swayny scornfully. "He means that's where you are at of course. Which is what I mean. We've arrived at Europe. That's the kind of a fast mail sled we are. In three minutes we've carried you up hill and down dale, over the sea to Europe."

"Really?" cried Jimmieboy, dumfounded.

"Certainly," said Swanny. "You are now in Europe. That blue place you see over on the right is Germany, off to the left is France and that little pink speck is Switzerland. See that glistening thing just on the edge of the pink speck?"

"Yes," said Jimmieboy.

"That's an Alp," said Swanny. "It's too bad we've got to get you home in time for breakfast. If we weren't in such a hurry, we'd let you off so that you could buy an Alp to take home to your brother. You could have snow-balls all through the summer if you had an Alp in your nursery, but we can't stop now to get it. We've got to runaway immediately. Ready Swayny?"

"Yes," said Swayny. "ALL ABOARD FOR ENGLAND. Passengers will please keep their seats until the sled comes to a standstill in the station."

And then they were off again.

"How did you like Europe?" asked Swanny, as they sped along through a beautiful country, which Swayny said was France.

"Very nice what I saw of it," said Jimmieboy. "But, of course I couldn't see very much in five minutes."

"Hoh! Hear that, Swayny?" said Swanny. "Couldn't see much in five minutes. Why you could see all Europe in five minutes, if you only looked fast enough. You kept your eye glued on that Alp, I guess."

"That's what he did," said Swayny. "And that's why it was so hard to get the sled started. I had to hump three times before I could get my runner off and it was all because he'd glued his eye on the Alp! Don't do it again, Jimmieboy. We haven't time to unglue your eye every time we start."

"I don't blame him," said Swanny "Those Alps are simply great, and I sometimes feel myself as if I'd like to look at 'em as much as forty minutes. I'd hate to be a hired man on an Alp, though."

"So would I," said Swayny. "It would be awful if the owner of the Alp made the

300

hired man shovel the snow off it every morning."

"I wasn't thinking of that so much as I was of getting up every morning, early, to push the clouds away," said Swanny. "People are very careless about their clouds on the Alps, and they wander here and there, straying from one man's lawn onto another's, just like cows where Jimmieboy lives. I knew a man once who bought the top of an Alp just for the view, and one of his neighbor's clouds came along and squatted down on his place and simply killed the view entirely, and I tell you he made his hired man's life miserable. Scolded him from morning until night, and fed him on cracked ice for a week, just because he didn't scare the cloud off when he saw it coming."

"I don't see how a man could scare a cloud off," said Jimmieboy.

301

"Easy as eating chocolate creams," said Swayny. "You can do it with a fan, if you have one big enough—but, I say, Swanny, put on the brakes there quick, or we'll run slam-bang into——"

"LONDON!" cried Swanny, putting on the brakes, and sure enough that's where they were. Jimmieboy knew it in a minute, because there was a lady coming out of a shop preceded by a band of music, and wearing a big crown on her head, whom he recognized at once as the great and good Queen, whose pictures he had often seen in his story books.

"Howdy do, little boy," said the Queen, as her eye rested on Jimmieboy.

"I'm very well, thank you, Ma'am," said Jimmieboy, holding out his hand for Her Majesty to shake.

"What are you doing here?" she asked.

"I'm sliding until breakfast is ready," he replied.

"Until breakfast is ready?" she cried. "Why, what time do you have breakfast?"

"Eight o'clock, so's papa can catch the 8:30 train, Ma'am," said Jimmieboy.

"But—it is now nearly one o'clock!" said the Queen.

"That's all right, Your Roily Highnishness," said Swanny. "This is an American boy and he breakfasts on the American plan. It isn't eight o'clock yet where he lives."

"Oh, yes—so it isn't," said the Queen. "I remember now. The sun rises earlier here than it does in America."

"Yes, Ma'am," put in Swayny. "It has to in order to get to America on time. America is some distance from here as you may have heard."

And before the Queen could say another word, the sled was sliding merrily along at such a rapid pace that Jimmieboy had to throw his arms about Swayny's neck to keep from falling overboard.

"W-where are we g-g gug-going to now?" he stammered.

"China," said Swanny.

"Egypt," said Swayny.

"I said China," cried Swanny, turning his eyes full upon Swayny and glaring at him.

"I know you did," said Swayny. "I may not show 'em, but I have ears. I, on the other hand said Egypt, and Egypt is where we are going. I want to show Jimmieboy the Pyramids. He's never seen a Pyramid and he has seen Chinamen."

"No doubt," said Swanny. "But this time he's not going to Egypt. I'm going to show him a Mandarin. He can build a

304

Pyramid with his blocks, but he never in his life could build a Mandarin. Therefore, Ho for China."

"You mean Bah! for China," said Swayny, angrily. "I'm not going to China, Mr. William G. Swanny and that's all there is about that. Last time I was there a Chinaman captured me and tied me to his pigtail and I vowed I'd never go again."

"And when I was in Egypt last time, I was stolen by a mummy, who wanted to broil and eat me because he hadn't had anything to eat for two thousand years. So I'm not going to Egypt."

Whereupon the two strange birds became involved in a dreadful quarrel, one trying to run the sled off toward China, the other trying, with equal vim, to steer it over to Egypt. The runners creaked; the red back groaned and finally there came a most dreadful crash. Swanny flew off with his runner to the land of Flowers, and Swayny, freed from his partner, forgetting Jimmieboy completely, sped on to Egypt.

And Jimmieboy.

Well, Jimmieboy, fell in between and by some great good fortune, for which I am not at all prepared to account, landed in a heap immediately beside his little bed in the nursery, not dressed in his furs at all but in his night gown, while out of doors not a speck of snow was to be seen, and strangest of all, when he was really dressed and had gone down stairs, there stood Magic and the two swan heads, as spick and span as you please, still waiting to be tried.

"HULLO!" SAID HIS PAPA. "WHERE HAVE YOU
BEEN?"—*See Page 157.*

THE STUPID LITTLE
APPLE-TREE

THE STUPID LITTLE
APPLE-TREE

JIMMIEBOY was playing in the orchard, and, as far as the birds and the crickets and the tumble-bugs could see, was as happy as the birds, as lively as the crickets, and as tumbly as the tumble-bugs. In fact, one of the crickets had offered to bet an unusually active tumble-bug that Jimmieboy could give him ten tumbles start and beat him five in a hundred, but the tumble-bug was a good little bug and wouldn't bet.

"I'm put here to tumble," said he. "That's my work in life, and I'm going to stick to it. Other creatures may be able to tumble better than I can, but that isn't going to make any difference to me. So long as I do the best I can, I'm satisfied. If you want to bet, go bet with the dandelions. They've got more gold in 'em than we tumble-bugs have."

Now, whether it was the sweet drowsiness of the afternoon, or the unusual number of tumbles he took on the soft, carpet-like grass in and out among the apple-trees, neither Jimmieboy nor I have ever been able to discover, but all of a sudden Jimmieboy thought it would be pleasant to rest awhile; and to accomplish this desirable end he could think of nothing better than to throw himself down at the foot of what he had always called the stupid little apple-tree. It was a very pretty tree, but it was always behind-time with its blossoms. All the other trees in the orchard burst out into bloom at the proper time, but the stupid little apple-tree, like a small boy in school who isn't as smart as some other boys, was never ready when the others were, and that was why Jimmieboy called it stupid.

"Jimmieboy! Jimmieboy!"

He turned about to see who had addressed him, but there was nothing in sight but a huge bumblebee, and he was entirely too busy at his daily stint to be wasting any time on Jimmieboy.

"Who are you? What do you want?" Jimmieboy asked.

"I'm—I'm a friend of yours," said the voice. "Oh, a splendid friend of yours, even if I am stupid. Do you want to earn an apple?"

"Yes," said Jimmieboy. "I'm very fond of apples—though I can get all I want without earning 'em."

"That's true enough," returned the voice; "but an apple you have given you isn't half so good as one you really earn all by yourself—that's why I want you to earn one. Of

311

course I'll give you all the apples I've got, anyhow, but I'd like to have you earn one of 'em, just to show you how much better it tastes because you have earned it."

"All right," said Jimmieboy, politely. "I'm very much obliged to you, and I'll earn it if you'll tell me how. But, I say," he added, "I can't see you—who are you?"

"Can't see me? That's queer," said the voice. "I'm right here—can't you see the stupid little apple-tree that's keeping the sun off you and stretching its arms up over you?"

"Yes," Jimmieboy replied. "I can see that, but I can't see you."

"Why, I'm it," said the voice. "It's the stupid little apple-tree that's talking to you. I'm me."

Jimmieboy sat up and looked at the tree with a surprised delight. "Oh! that's it, eh?" he said. "You can talk, can you?"

" Certainly," said the tree. " You didn't think we poor trees stood out here year in and year out, in cold weather and in warm, in storm and in sunshine, never lying down, always standing, without being allowed to talk, did you? That would be dreadfully cruel. It's bad enough not to be able to move around. Think how much worse it would be if we had to keep silent all that time! You can judge for yourself what a fearfully dull time we would have of it when you consider how hard it is for you to sit still in school for an hour without speaking."

" I just simply can't do it," said Jimmieboy. " That's the only thing my teacher don't like about me. She says I'm movey and loquacious."

" I don't know what loquacious means," said the tree.

" Neither do I," said Jimmieboy, " but I

313

guess it has something to do with talking too much when you hadn't ought to. But tell me, Mr. Tree, how can I earn the apple? "

" Don't be so formal," said the tree. " Don't call me Mr. Tree. You've known me long enough to be more intimate."

" Very well," said Jimmieboy. " I'll call you whatever you want me to. What shall I call you? "

" Call me Stoopy," said the tree, softly. " Stoopy for short. I always liked that name."

Jimmieboy laughed. " It's an awful funny name," he said. " Stoopy! Ha-ha-ha! What's it short for? "

" Stupid," said the tree. " That is, while it's quite as long as Stupid, it seems shorter. Anyhow, it's more affectionate, and that's why I want you to call me by it."

" Very well, Stoopy," said Jimmieboy.

314

"Now, about the apple. Have you got it with you?"

"No," returned the tree. "But I'm making it, and it's going to be the finest apple you ever saw. It will have bigger, redder cheeks than any other apple in the world, and it'll have a core in it that will be just as good to eat as marmalade, and it'll be all for you if you'll do something for me to-morrow."

"I'll do it if I can," said Jimmieboy.

"Of course—that's what I mean," said Stoopy. "Nobody can do a thing he can't do; and if you find that you can't do it, don't do it; you'll get the apple just the same, only you won't have earned it, and it may not seem so good, particularly the core. I suppose you know that to-morrow is Decoration Day?"

"Yes, indeed," said Jimmieboy. "Mamma's going to send a lot of flowers to the

315

Committee, and papa's going to take me to see the soldiers, and after that I'm going over to the semingary to see them decorate the graves."

"That's what I thought," said the tree, with a sigh. "I wish I could go. There's nothing I'd like to do better than to go over there and drop a lot of blossoms around on the graves of the men who went to war and lost their lives so that you might have a country, and we trees could grow in peace without being afraid of having a cannon-ball shot into us, cutting us in two—but I want to tell you a little story about all that. You didn't know I was planted by a little boy who went to the war and got killed, did you?"

"No," returned Jimmieboy, softly. "I didn't know that. I asked papa one day who planted you, and he said he guessed you just grew."

" Well, that's true, I did just grow," said Stoopy, " but I had to be planted first, and I was planted right here by a little boy only ten years old. He was awfully good to me, too. He used to take care of me just as if I were a little baby. I wasn't more than half as tall as he was when he set me out here, and I was his tree, and he was proud as could be to feel that he owned me; and he used to tell me that when I grew big and had apples he was going to sell the apples and buy nice things for his mother with the money he got for 'em. We grew up together. He took such good care of me that I soon got to be taller than he was, and the taller I became the prouder he was of me. Oh, he was a fine boy, Jimmieboy, and as he grew up his mother and father were awfully proud of him. And then the war broke out. He was a little over twenty years old then, and he couldn't be kept from going to fight. He

317

joined the regiment that was raised here, and after a little while he said good-by to his mother and father, and then he came out here to me and put his arms around my trunk and kissed me good-by too, and he plucked a little sprig of leaves from one of my branches and put it in his buttonhole, and then he went away. That was the last time I saw him. He was killed in his first battle."

Here Stoopy paused for an instant, and trembled a little, and a few blossoms fell like trickling tear-drops, and fluttered softly to the ground.

"They brought him home and buried him out there in the semingary," the tree added, "and that was the end of it. His father and mother didn't live very long after that, and then there wasn't anybody to take care of his grave any more. When that happened, I made up my mind that I'd do what I could;

318

but around here all the apple-blossoms are withered and gone by the time Decoration Day comes, and nobody would take plain leaves like mine to put on a soldier's grave, so I began to put off blossoming until a little later than the other trees, and that's how I came to be called the stupid little apple-tree. Nobody knew why I did it, but I did, and so I didn't mind being called stupid. I was doing it all for him, and every year since then I've been late, but on Decoration Day I've always had blossoms ready. The trouble has been, though, that nobody has ever come for 'em, and I've had all my work and trouble so far for nothing. It's been a great disappointment."

"I see," said Jimmieboy, softly. "What you want me to do is to take some of your blossoms over there to-morrow and put 'em —put 'em where you want 'em put."

"That's it, that's it!" cried the stupid

little apple-tree, eagerly. "Oh, if you only will, Jimmieboy!"

"Indeed I will," said Jimmieboy. "I'll come here in the morning and gather up the blossoms, and take every one you have ready over in a basket, and I'll get papa to find out where your master's grave is, and he'll have every one of them."

"Thank you, thank you," returned Stoopy; "and you'll find that all I've said about your apple will come true, and after this I'll be *your* tree forever and forever."

Jimmieboy was about to reply, when an inconsiderate tumble-bug tripped over his hand, which lay flat on the grass, and in an instant all of the boy's thoughts on the subject fled from his mind, and he found himself sitting up on the grass, gazing sleepily about him. He knew that he had probably been dreaming, although he is by no means certain that that was the case, for,

320

as if to remind him of his promise, as he started to rise, a handful of blossoms loosened by the freshening evening breezes came fluttering down into his lap, and the little lad resolved that, dream or no dream, he would look up the whereabouts of the young soldier-boy's grave, and would decorate it with apple-blossoms, and these from the stupid little apple-tree only.

And that is why one long-forgotten soldier's grave in the cemetery across the hills back of Jimmieboy's house was white and sweetly fragrant with apple-blossoms when the sun had gone down upon Decoration Day.

As for the stupid little apple-tree, it is still at work upon the marvelously red-cheeked apple which Jimmieboy is to claim as his reward.

Reprint Publishing

FOR PEOPLE WHO GO FOR ORIGINALS.

This book is a facsimile reprint of the original edition. The term refers to the facsimile with an original in size and design exactly matching simulation as photographic or scanned reproduction.

Facsimile editions offer us the chance to join in the library of historical, cultural and scientific history of mankind, and to rediscover.

The books of the facsimile edition may have marks, notations and other marginalia and pages with errors contained in the original volume. These traces of the past refers to the historical journey that has covered the book.

ISBN 978-3-95940-053-4

Facsimile reprint of the original edition
Copyright © 2015 Reprint Publishing
All rights reserved.

www.reprintpublishing.com